AN Insane LOVE 3

A NOVEL BY

BIANCA

© 2018 Royalty Publishing House

Published by Royalty Publishing House
www.royaltypublishinghouse.com

ALL RIGHTS RESERVED
Any unauthorized reprint or use of the material is prohibited. No part of this book may be reproduced or transmitted in any form or by any means, electronic or mechanical, including photocopying, recording, or by any information storage without express permission by the author or publisher. This is an original work of fiction. Names, characters, places and incidents are either products of the author's imagination or are used fictitiously and any resemblance to actual persons, living or dead, is entirely coincidental.
Contains explicit language & adult themes suitable for ages 16+ only.

Royalty Publishing House is now accepting manuscripts from aspiring or experienced urban romance authors!

WHAT MAY PLACE YOU ABOVE THE REST:

Heroes who are the ultimate book bae: strong-willed, maybe a little rough around the edges but willing to risk it all for the woman he loves.

Heroines who are the ultimate match: the girl next door type, not perfect - has her faults but is still a decent person. One who is willing to risk it all for the man she loves.

The rest is up to you! Just be creative, think out of the box, keep it sexy and intriguing!

If you'd like to join the Royal family, send us the first 15K words (60 pages) of your completed manuscript to submissions@royaltypublishinghouse.com

SYNOPSIS

Taiwan has finally gotten her freedom and her life back, or so she thinks. After learning more about Frank and his troubled life, she becomes more connected to him than ever. Romero is not one who likes to lose. Romero is not backing down and will do whatever he has to do to get Taiwan back, even if it means taking away the people that she's closest to.

Frank's childhood trauma is coming back to haunt him in more ways than one. The last straw is when his trauma causes him to almost hurt someone who he cares about deeply, prompting him to go underground to handle his business and get himself together. When he finally has a grip on his life, another dark secret is revealed, changing his life altogether.

Rubee finds herself devastated after the sudden disappearance of Bash. Kade, fed up with feeling like Rubee is confused about what she wants, makes the decision easy for her. Will Rubee get it together before she loses the best thing that has happened to her and Raylee?

In this explosive, drama-filled finale, devastating secrets are revealed, family ties are severed, and love is put on the line.

PREVIOUSLY IN AN INSANE LOVE 2

Frank

*A*fter the meeting, I went back to Mayhem's house with him. I wasn't ready to go home yet. Everything was still too fresh, and Mayhem didn't want me to be there alone with my thoughts. He already knew that I was on some murderous type shit. I was ready for anybody to find that bitch, Alex, and I swear I was going to pop her fucking head off her shoulders. A part of me wanted to make her suffer, and a part of me wanted to beat her mothafuckin' ass as if she was a nigga.

Mayhem went into the house with Olena and his kids, and I was headed toward the guesthouse where Taiwan was. This morning, I stared at her naked body and felt like a piece of shit. That shit fucked with me so bad knowing that I caused her pain and for no fucking reason. I was just glad that she understood, because that was all I knew how to do when people pissed me off; make them feel pain. I admit that I overreacted sometimes, and I was trying to change that, but people just be trying me. Mayhem had been trying to get me to try therapy, but I didn't have time to be sitting down, telling no quack ass nigga my business. He'd have me locked up, thinking that my life story was made up, so I was good on that. I'd just lost Alex, but as long as I had Mayhem, I was straight. That was all I needed. He was all I needed. I knew for a fact that he'd never switch up on me.

When I walked into the guesthouse and into the bedroom, Taiwan was laid across the bed, naked, listening to music. Kem's voice crooned through the speaker. She was so focused on her iPad in front of her that she didn't even know that I had come into the room. I noticed that she was squeezing her thighs together, making me lick my lips. Her body was so damn beautiful, and I couldn't get enough of looking at her.

"There's nowhere to hide when love is calling your name," I sang along with Kem, getting her attention.

She whipped her head around toward me and was looking at me crazy as I continued to sing with Kem.

"Wow… I finally know something that you can't do, and that's sing. Leave that to the professionals."

"Aye, don't make me go find a singing coach because I'll do it," I told her.

I kicked my shoes off and lay next to her, and I started to smell *her*. The reason that she was clenching her thighs together.

"Why are you wet, Tai?" I asked her.

"How did you know that I was wet?" She eyed me.

"I smell her. It's turning me on."

"Well, I was reading this book, *Adored by a New York Drug Lord*, by Tya Marie, and this sex scene between the two main characters is kind of hot," she admitted.

"Hold on. You letting a nigga in a book—"

"His name is Urban."

"Whatever his name is, getting you wet, and you got a real live dick that you can get any time you want. I'm jealous like a mothafucka," I told her and climbed between her legs while she was still laying on her stomach reading. I pushed her right leg up so her pussy lips could open right up, and her shit was sopping wet. "So that nigga Urban got your pussy wet, huh? Let me see if I can top that nigga. Arch your back and poke that pussy out to me. Read what he doing while I feast on this wet ass pussy."

"Frank…" she moaned when I ran my tongue down her slit. "Oh my God, you're going to hurt your—"

"Be quiet about my arm, and read to me while I eat," I told her.

She didn't lie, because this shit was uncomfortable. I took my sling off and threw it next to us. I was able to lie flat on my stomach now and use both of my hands to press down on her lower back to make sure she kept that mothafucka arched. I dived into her pussy, and she tasted so damn good, especially since it tasted like she had already came on herself.

"I-I-nodded mutely, unable to take anything more at the feeling of that same magical tongue flicking at my clit…" she read and paused.

I started flicking the tip of my tongue on her hardened clit, and she kept trying to run, but I had my hands in the right place. Her ass was stuck on my tongue… because I was running my tongue up and down her ass and then stopping back on her clit.

"Keep reading." I growled and smacked her on her ass.

"I could do nothing but lay back with my eyes crossed, clenching my thighs around… around his head until I felt another orgasm coming. I tried pushing him… Frankkkkk… I tried pushing him away… shit… but Urban wasn't having that."

Her nut was seeping out of her, and I kept making love to her pussy lips. She managed to break free from my hold and fall flat to the bed, so I reached for her arms, pulled them between her legs, and kept eating. She couldn't do shit in the position she was in but take this tongue lashing. Her pussy lips were starting to swell, which meant I was doing my damn job. Her freak nasty ass started to twerk on my tongue, and I loved that shit, so I snaked my long tongue inside of her, and she lost it. She started throwing her pussy back on my tongue.

"Frank… oh my God!" she groaned.

After she had cum again, I let her arms go, and she fell flat on the bed again. I rolled over on my back and gripped her waist with my good arm and pulled her on my lap. I pulled my pants to the middle of my thighs and freed my hard ass dick. She lifted up a little and eased down on my dick until I filled her walls to capacity. We both groaned with pleasure. Taiwan placed her feet flat on the bed and started riding my shit slowly, and it felt fucking amazing. She was coming all the way up to the head of my dick, and then sliding down slowly, making sure to clench her walls all the way down. I looked at her coating my dick with her beautiful cream and then looked back up at her, and she wore a beautiful look of pleasure on her face. I lifted my good arm up and gripped her neck. She gripped my arm with both hands and started riding my shit like I was a bull. I thrust upward so I could give her everything that I had to give.

"Ohhhh, Franklin," she whispered, and my dick got harder. Taiwan's head was rolling around like she was in a whole different world.

"Sereni-fucking-ty. Don't fucking call my name like that, girl. Shit! You got my dick harder than it's ever been."

"Franklin... your piercings are hitting my... oh shit... Franklin..."

"Look at me..." I urged her.

She looked down at me and bit her lip so hard that I thought she was going to bite that mothafucka off.

"Have my baby, Serenity," I told her. "Shit, have my baby, woman. Can I get you pregnant, bae?" I sounded so fucking desperate.

"Yes, Franklin. Cum in me. I need to feel you," she said, looking directly into my eyes.

It was at this moment that our souls tied, and she would be mine forever. I could see the love she had for me in her eyes. She was meeting every thrust, and I could feel the nut shooting through the head of my dick. I was cumming hard as fuck inside of her.

"Oh my God! I feel you, Franklin," she whispered and leaned forward to lay on my chest.

Our hearts were beating so fast against each other.

"We have to be somewhere in a few hours, bae, but we gotta catch a nap first, aight?"

"Yes, baby daddy," she said and kissed my chin.
Baby daddy? That shit sounds good.

Three hours later

Taiwan and I woke up about two hours ago, but I had to take her body for another spin. I had become addicted to her, and she just didn't know it. I told her that I was addicted to her, and I hoped she knew what came with that. She said she understood as long as I didn't lock her in that room again. I told her that as long as she kept it trill with me, she would never see that room again. In the shower, I fucked her… again. My baby mama's shit was so swollen, but she kept getting wet for me, and she kept throwing that shit back. Now, this was something that I could get used to; fucking every time my dick got hard. Her lil' wild ass loved when I made my piercings hit her g-spot. When we got out of the shower, I fucked her on the sink. After I made her squirt, she said that we were done for real that time. We got cleaned up again and headed out of the guesthouse. I was walking behind Taiwan, and her ass was walking gapped legged like a mothafucka, but she was trying to hide it. Before I opened the door for Taiwan, Mayhem told me that he needed to holler at me about something, and I told him that it wouldn't take long. I was going to go holla at Miguel and Emmanuel, give them some water and food, and then take my baby mama out for a late lunch date.

Taiwan and I were holding hands the whole way to my other crib.

"If I'm gon' be something to you, then you are going to have to get rid of that," she said to me, referring to Alex's name being etched into my skin.

"Mane, I can't wait to get this shit covered up. What you think I should get?"

"Serenity. Not for my name, but because every time you look at it, you'll think of peace... and me," she whispered that last part.

"Yeah, aight Ms. *Not For My Name.*"

Twenty minutes later, we pulled into my crib. I got the water out of the trunk and walked to doors of the cellar.

"This your house, too?" she asked.

"Yeah, why?" I asked her.

"It's so far out. What do you use it for?"

"You about to see."

I grabbed my key and opened the door. I let her walk down the stairs before me, and I shut the cellar doors behind me. I handed her the water bottles and took my phone out of my pocket to turn the music and lights off. I typed the code to the door and lifted them slowly. I went first and then helped Taiwan down the stairs. She gasped when she saw Emmanuel and Miguel in the cages.

"Franklin... these are my friends!" she hissed and ran over to Miguel first, but he was passed out.

"We about to see if they are really your friends," I told her.

I grabbed my cymbals that were on the floor and started banging them together, waking them right up.

"Rise and shine, gentlemen!" I spoke to them as they were starting to wake up.

I walked over to Miguel first, and he looked terrible but not as bad as he smelled.

"Listen, Miguel, apparently, my baby mama is really fond of you, so I'm going to give you a chance to talk first. Here..." I said, snatching the water out of Taiwan's hand. "I have a bottle of water. You only have one chance, and I mean *only* one chance to spare your life for four more days. Oh, and just so you won't get any cues from the fat boy..." I said and paused.

I took my phone out of my pocket, typed on it for a few seconds, and moments later, a completely steel wall fell around his cage.

"He can't hear anything which means whatever you say will be between me and you, okay?"

He nodded his head sheepishly.

"Frank, this is not right. This is torture; he's been nothing but nice to me," she said to me.

I opened the cage, and he fell out and on the floor. I squatted and took his tape off his mouth.

"Now, speak!"

"What... what do you want to know?" he whispered and started coughing from having a very dry throat.

"Anything you want to tell me. I'm all ears," I said.

I gave him a sip of water, and he acted like it was a B12 shot.

"My uncle... has no intentions on ever letting Taiwan go. I tried to tell him to leave her alone, but... but he wouldn't listen. He's... he's selfish. Very. He's been trying to find information on you, Frank. He's obsessed with you," Miguel admitted.

"Really? Why?"

He nodded his head toward Taiwan. "Because she's obsessed with you."

I looked up at Taiwan, and she looked mortified, and I winked at her, making her turn her head away from us. I gave him two sips of water.

"How does he know that?"

"He found her journal last year."

"Oh my God! I completely forgot about that!" she said and palmed her forehead.

"Miguel, how do you feel about Taiwan?"

"Franklin!" she hissed.

"She's beautiful. Very, very beautiful. Smart. Funny. Caring. I wanted her to leave him. I want to leave him, but once you're in the cartel, you in there for life," he groaned from pain.

"One last question, Miguel. Am I going to have to kill Romero?"

He nodded his head before having a coughing fit. "He doesn't like to lose, Frank. The night of Taiwan's party, we were supposed to snatch her."

"And you're down with that?"

"No. I want her happy. She wasn't happy with him anymore."

My eyebrow went up, and I chuckled.

"Awwee, Miguel, you're in love with my woman, and I get it. Her pussy so fucking tight and she gets really fucking wet, I tell ya."

"Franklinnnnn." Taiwan groaned, but I ignored her and continued to glare at him.

"That's exactly how she sounds when she getting ready to... You know what? Never mind. But when you see her, know... know! Know! Know! Know that, that's me. Now, I'm going to give her this bottle of water and let her finish letting you sip it. Depends on how I feel after I talk to the fat boy over there, I might go upstairs and make you some grits or something. Something that'll stick to you," I told him and patted his head.

I handed Taiwan the bottle of water and then lifted the steel cage off the fat boy. I took my key and opened his cage. He fell out, and I saw a look of anger in his eyes.

"Your wound healed nicely. You feel like talking?" I asked him.

I squatted and took the duct tape off his mouth, and he started shouting in a different language, making me look at him with a crazy look on my face.

Placing my hand over my heart, with wide eyes, I stared at him with a very sarcastic, sad look on my face. "Emmanuel, why are you so angry? You were a comedian four days ago, but today—"

He continued to speak in his language.

"Oh Miguelllyyy, is this fat boy calling me racial slurs?" I asked him.

Miguel nodded his head up and down slowly. "In Italian."

"Hold that thought, fatty."

I took my phone out my pocket and went on the internet.

"Google translate," I said while typing. "Italian," I whispered. "Now, say that again." I held the phone to his mouth, but he spat on the phone and continued talking, and it was picking up some of his words.

"Slow down. You're going too fast. Whoa. Monkey. Porch Monkey.

Kill. Bitch. Blacky." I turned my phone off and put it back in my pocket. "Those were really mean words, Emmanuel. No water for you, and just for that, you get to watch your partner over here drink water and eat grits. I bet your fat ass love grits too."

I put the tape back over his mouth, picked him up, and put him back in the cage. I shut the door with a smile on my face.

"Can he have that bottle of water too?" Taiwan asked.

"Nah," I said and stuffed the bottle of water in my pocket.

I went upstairs and made him some quick grits and came back downstairs. I let Taiwan feed him.

"This could have been you, fatty, but nah. You had to be mean, so now you die a slow and painful death," I said to Emmanuel.

After Taiwan finished feeding him, I set the bowl on the floor next to the cage.

Knocking Miguel against the head with my knuckles, I said, "Look, I'm going to put you in the slightly bigger cage. It's a bucket in there where you can sit down. I'mma also give you some earplugs. I'll be back in a couple of days. Cool?"

He nodded his head slowly.

"I want to stay over here, so I'll help. Anything you need me to do, I'll do it," Miguel whispered.

"Keep it that way."

I helped him up, put the tape back over his mouth, and put him in the bigger cage. He immediately sat down and laid against the rails. I put the ear plugs in his ear, and he nodded his head to me. I closed and locked the cage. I hoped that nigga wasn't lying because I was going to need all the help I could get if I were going to take out a nigga that was in the fucking Cartel.

Forty-five minutes later

Me and my baby mama were now sitting in a slightly crowded restaurant, and she had been quiet the whole time, ever since we left my crib out in the woods. I wanted her to say what was on her mind, but she kept ignoring me, but I wasn't going to keep pressuring her. I tried to touch her hands, but she moved them back.

"Taiwan, I'm sorry if you don't like the way I do things, but that is how I get answers. You think Miguel would have told me that had he not been locked in there for all those hours?" I told her. "Look at me... I don't do that shit to no one who doesn't deserve it... Don't look at me like that; you were a mistake. An overreaction."

"An overreaction, Franklin? I'm not worried about Miguel or Emmanuel. You told me this morning that you wanted me to have your kid, and even been calling me your baby mama, but I can't have kids with someone who thinks that locking someone in a room for days and starving them to get answers is the right way to do things. My only concern is that you'll lock our child—"

"Stop!" I growled and banged my fist on the table. Talking about my childhood was always a soft spot for me, and that was why I had only talked about it once. It sent me into a horrible flashback. "My kids will have a great relationship with me... with us, to the point that they will talk to us about everything bothering them. They won't have to lie to me about anything. I'll treat them like fucking kids, and they will have a normal fucking life. They will go outside, play, and get dirty and shit like normal kids. I won't lock them in the house, making them learn how to fight, and—"

"Franklin, come back to me," Taiwan whispered and grabbed my hands.

I blinked my eyes and looked down at my hands shaking inside of her small ones. Embarrassed, I snatched my hands from her and hid my hands under the table. I couldn't even look Tai in her eyes.

"Franklin, where did you go? Did you go to your childhood?" she softly asked.

"I don't want to talk about it. Please just leave it alone. I can't..."

"Okay, whenever you ready to talk, I'm ready to listen. I won't judge you, okay? Look at me, baby daddy."

I cut my eyes at her, and she smiled at me while giving me a reassuring nod. I didn't know when I'd be able to talk to her about her about my childhood, but to know that she was willing to wait really made a nigga feel good. Her eyes kept darting from me to someone or something else."

Immediately, I went to my waist. "Who do you see, Tai?"

She leaned in and whispered, "Alicia, that FBI agent I was telling you about. What if she has been following us?"

"She hasn't. I always watch my back when I'm out rolling. She finna come over here?" I asked her. "Stop looking over there. You looking nervous and shit."

"Shit, she's coming over here."

I flipped my shirt back over my gun, just as the woman approached the table.

"Hey, Taiwan… interesting to see you here. Do you have a moment so we can chat?" she asked her, and she looked at me.

Alicia was a short white lady that worked for the Feds. I wasn't going to let her talk to Taiwan alone. She looked at me—stared at me—longer than usual until I raised my eyebrow, and she looked back at Taiwan. Her face was turning red and shit, and it was making me nervous. Taiwan noticed it too, but if she didn't say anything, I was going to let it rock too.

I shook my head. "Nah, shorty. Whatever you got to say to my baby mama, you can say it right here."

"Taiwan, I think you are in danger, and it's best that we put you in Witness—"

"Bitch, please, I'm her Witness Protection."

"Sir, you don't… you don't understand who you're dealing with."

"Nah, he doesn't understand who *he's* dealing with. We are good. You just better make sure that you and your team be ready to collect all those cocker spaniel ass niggas up off the street."

"Please… just think about it," Alicia begged.

She handed Taiwan her card, but I snatched it right up out of her hand and ripped it up. She left the table, and I watched her until she disappeared out the door.

My phone vibrated in my pocket, and I took it out to see who was texting me. It was from an unknown number.

Unknown: *I think it's time that we had a conversation about my bitch, and my family members you're harboring... Chaz Alphonso Bourne.*

-Tag! Now, you're it.
Romero Santiago

FRANK

I kept staring at the text message that came across my phone. My skin started to grow warm because of the adrenaline that was flowing through my blood. My heart began to beat faster than normal because Romero had more pull than I expected him to have because this cocker spaniel ass nigga called me by Chaz. I hadn't been called Chaz since I was fourteen years old, and I'm thirty-six years old now. For some odd reason, him calling me Chaz could mean a lot of things, but what? Could he know my parents or their real names? Who else knew my family well enough to give him that information? To my knowledge, the only other person that knew my parents was Rickey, and that nigga was dead. I knew for a fact that nigga was dead because I watched Korupt push his body into a fire to cremate him. I could feel myself getting ready to zone out.

"Franklin!" Taiwan hissed.

I blinked my eyes a few times and focused on my beautiful woman across the table from me.

"I've been calling your name for the last five minutes. Who texted you, and why are you looking like that?"

"Like what?"

"Your eyes. They did something. Your pupils were dilating. It was like you dozed off with your eyes open. Is everything okay?"

"Actually, no. We have to go."

"What do you mean we have to go? We haven't even gotten our food yet, Franklin. Tell me what is going on," Taiwan stressed, but I couldn't tell her… not yet.

I had to get her home so I could let Mayhem know that this shit with Alex was going to have to be pushed to the backburner. I went into my wallet and pulled a crisp one-hundred-dollar bill out and placed it on the table. Grabbing a fuming Taiwan by her elbow, I lifted her out of the seat and started pulling her toward the door.

"Act natural, bae, please," I told her.

Taiwan and I walked out of the door, hand in hand like we were a perfect couple. I opened the door for her and looked around while walking around to my side of the car. Romero was going to die, and soon.

"Baby, can you tell me what that was about? I'm getting scared. It's Romero, isn't it? It was him that texted you, right?" Taiwan asked as I was dipping through the streets at unsafe speeds. "I'll go back, Franklin. He's never going to leave me alone, and I don't want you or Mayhem to get hurt behind me. I'll just go back," she whispered, and it pissed me all the way off.

"Mane, you don't got faith in me, huh? You don't got faith in me that I'll murk that bitch ass nigga, and we can live happily ever after."

I looked at her, and she was looking straight ahead. "Taiwan! Fucking look at me, goddamn it!" I yelled and banged my fist against the steering wheel.

I was getting pissed off. She turned her head slightly toward me, and tears were sliding down her face. I didn't give a fuck about her tears at the moment. She could cry me a fucking river; I didn't give one fuck.

"Mane, get the fuck on with them tears, mothafucka. I feel like you want to go back to that nigga anyway. If you do, you can call that nigga right now, and take your ass back to Italy with that nigga. I'll let you out right here on the side of this highway."

"Frank, why are you talking to me like this? I don't want you to get hurt. Is it a fucking crime to give a fuck about you and your wellbeing?"

"What the fuck does that have to do with anything, Taiwan? You going back to that nigga ain't gon' stop that nigga from trying to kill me because he knows as long as I'm alive, I ain't going to stop fucking with you. You'll never see anybody you claim you love again if you go back to Italy. Is that what you want?"

She started waving her hands dramatically in front of her. "No, that's not what I—"

"Well fucking act like it, damn!" I hissed.

Once we pulled up to a red light, I turned and looked at her. "Come here!" I ordered her.

She leaned over in the seat, and I caught her by her cheeks with my free hand and squeezed them together. "And don't you ever in your fuckin' life doubt me again, Taiwan. Am I understood?"

"You… are… hurting…"

Squeezing tighter, I growled, "You better answer my mothafuckin' question."

"Ye-yes," she stuttered.

I kissed her lips and let her go. She fell back against the seat with an attitude and started rubbing her jaws. In my rearview mirror, I could see a black jeep creeping up on the side of me. It was another car right next to me, so they couldn't get directly beside to me. Slowly, I reached for my pistol that was on my side and put it on my lap.

"Baby girl, reach into the console and get that gun," I told her while keeping my eye on the jeep.

Doing as she was told, she pulled the gun from the door and placed it on her lap.

"You know how to shoot?" I asked her, praying that I got the right answer.

"Yeah, somewhat. I'm not a professional or any—"

"Good enough. Check the clip and cock the gun for me."

"Frank, what is—"

"Ssshhhhh. Shit about to get really ugly in these Chicago streets, shorty. Just know that."

My windows were tinted way past the legal limit, so they couldn't see in here. My whole car was bulletproof, so I wasn't worried about them shooting me. Taiwan did as I told her, and I took the gun from her and put it next to me.

"Now reach in the back and get that big gun that's on the floor," I instructed her.

Chicago lights were long enough to get you murked for real if you weren't careful. Taiwan handed me my semi-automatic gun, and looking at the full clip made a nigga smile like a mothafucka. Once the light turned green, I slowly pulled off, fully knowing exactly what the jeep was going to do. They sped up to get right next to me. The passenger side windows came down, and two niggas started blasting at the side of my car.

Blocka! Blocka! Blocka!

Taiwan screamed as they started lighting the side of my car up. They sped up and started lighting my windshield window up. Taiwan was ducking and screaming like a mothafucka. If I wasn't trained for shit like this, I would have been screwed.

Blocka! Blocka! Blocka!

"Baby, calm down! Shit! Shit! Shit! Calm down!" I shouted at her. "Taiwan, take the wheel!"

"WHAT!" she shouted.

"Baby, take the fucking wheel! Hold it straight as you can," I instructed her.

"I can't! I can't! I can't! I can't!" she screamed as the bullets continued to hit the car.

The more the bullets hit the window, the more my view became obstructed.

"Mama, I got faith in you!"

The bullets ceased, which meant they were either reloading or out of bullets. I cocked my semi-automatic, let the window down, and took a deep breath. I put Taiwan's hand on the wheel, forcing her to hold it. I stuck my gun and head out of the window and started letting that shit sound off. My bullets were specially made, so they were penetrating anything. I ain't no fool.

Tat-tat-tat-tat-tat-tat-tat-tat-tat-tat-tat-tat

I was letting that bitch sound off, and I was fucking that jeep up. I bust the back tires, and they started swerving in the jeep. I took my hand off the trigger just for a second to give them bitch ass niggas time to get back out the window, and the dude in the back must have thought I was done because as soon as he stuck his head out the window, I let my shit sound off again.

Tat-tat-tat-tat-tat-tat-tat-tat-tat-tat

Their tires were shooting out sparks now, which meant the jeep was about to stop any minute. I got back in the car and set the gun down next to me. I grabbed my pistol and stuck my head back out the window.

Pop!

"FRANK!" Taiwan shouted.

I let out a low whistle. "Whew!"

I got back in the car fast as shit. That nigga shot my goddamn hat off my head.

"Oh my God, I thought you were—"

"That was my favorite fucking hat," I growled.

I grabbed my semi-automatic again, got back out the window again, and started letting that bitch sound off.

Tat-tat-tat-tat-tat-tat-tat-tat.

That time I shot the dude in the passenger seat, and I managed to hit the gas tank as well, making the truck catch fire and flip twice in the air before landing on its roof. I got back in the car and took the wheel from Taiwan. I pulled about ten feet behind the car.

"Wait right here," I ordered her.

I grabbed my pistol and walked over to the burning jeep. Burning flesh had never bothered me. I dragged the driver out of the truck and over in the grass. I stood over him and watched him as he struggled to breathe. He had two bullet wounds in his abdomen.

"It seems like Romero really underestimated who I was, huh?" I queried, knowing if he tried to speak, he would choke even harder on his own blood.

A phone started ringing in his shirt pocket. He slowly raised his hand to get it but put his hand back down. He was using all of the energy he had left to breathe.

"You don't mind if I get that, do you?" I asked him. "I'm sure you don't."

I slid the phone out of his pocket and answered it.

"Is it done?" the guy said into the phone.

I didn't say anything because I wanted to listen to the background.

"Anthony, is it done? Tell me that black Scarface wannabe is finished," the guy growled into the phone.

I cocked my gun.

"It is now," I spoke into the phone.

Pow!

I popped Anthony in his head and put him out of his misery.

"You black bitch!" he hissed into the phone.

"Romero, you gotta be quicker than that. Now that amateur night is over with, I'm going to go soak my achy fingers and then dip my black Scarface wannabe dick inside of Taiwan's pussy."

The angry growl he let out made me laugh. He started spewing out a lot of shit in Italian.

"Now, don't go being mean, Romero. If you leave me alone, I'll leave you alone. You keep coming, it's going to get worse. Bye bye now," I said and hung up on him still speaking in Italian.

I got back in the car, and Taiwan was sitting completely still, looking out the cracked windshield. I scooted my seat back and kicked my windshield out, making Taiwan jump. The whole way toward Mayhem's house, she was quiet as a church mouse, so I grabbed her hand to reassure her that she would be okay.

"Tai, please say something to me," I said to her.

"Y-yo-yo-you are a killer," she stuttered lowly.

"Well, yeah, but you knew that though."

She didn't say anything else until we were pulling in the gate of Mayhem's house. As soon as I put the car in park, Mayhem came busting out of his front door and toward my car. I got out the car and walked around the car to open the door for Taiwan, and she rushed by me and into the house.

"We need to talk!" both Mayhem and I said at the same time.

"You first," we both said in unison again.

After a few moments of silence, Mayhem said, "Explain what the fuck happened to your car," he said and started walking around my car, assessing the damage.

"Long story short, Romero had some niggas slide down on Tai and me, and they started blasting at me."

"You murked them niggas?"

"Nigga, what's my name? You know them niggas sleep! The long story is that Fed bitch ran up on me and Taiwan while we were about to eat, talking about she was going to put Taiwan in Witness Protection and shit. I told that bitch to get lost because I'm Taiwan's Witness Protection, but after all of that, I got this message."

I pulled my phone out of my pocket and showed Mayhem the fucking text message that Romero sent to my phone.

"Nigga, that shit with Alex is going to have to be put on hold, because we have to get rid of this nigga. I'm not going to be able to sleep at night until this nigga is dead."

"Not quite. How is your arm? You don't have on your sling," Mayhem asked me.

"All the adrenaline is running through my body, so I don't feel shit. I'll probably put it back on later, but what the fuck you mean 'not quite'?"

"Maybe you should come inside and sit down for a second while I explain to you—"

"Nope, I don't feel like sitting down, bruh. Talk to me."

"Well, you remember when Rubee called me earlier?"

"Yeah, but headline this story for me because I want to go inside and check on Taiwan. I know she shook right now and shit, but—"

"Bash and Alex were talking, and Kharisma may have had something to do with it."

I grabbed the bridge of my nose and let out a low chuckle. "Sebastian? Sebastian as in Rubee's boyfriend and Raylee's dad. Sebastian as in the dude that works for us?"

Mayhem slowly nodded his head, while I laughed maniacally.

"Franklin." Mayhem called my name as soon as I started walking to my broke down car.

"Franklin… he already in the wind, and so is Kharisma," Mayhem informed me as soon as I put my hand on my door handle.

"See, while you and Taiwan were gone, I started putting shit together. Rubee met Sebastian right around the time that Alex met you. Of course, I pulled the text messages, and they were in a full-blown relationship. I have them in the house if you want to read them."

I put my back against the car and slid down to the ground. My parents would be so disappointed in me. How could I have not seen the snake in that bitch's eyes? I always had a gut feeling about that nigga Bash, but I would have never pegged it to be that he was fucking around with Alex. See, I had a gut feeling when we were in the store and both of them were in my presence, but I shrugged that shit off.

"Fuck! Fuck! Fuck!" I groaned while banging the back of my head against the car door.

Mayhem came around the car and looked at me. He slid down next to me and stared out at his large ass yard.

"Franklin, you wouldn't have known. She hid that shit well," Mayhem said.

"Nah, I vetted that bitch. Kharisma nor Bash was nowhere in the report. Bruh, I'm sick to my fucking stomach. Mayhem, when I get my hands on that bitch, I'mma choke her until her eyeballs pop out of her mothafuckin' head."

"I feel you, bro. Kharisma got it coming. Her little son about to be a fucking orphan. I don't even know where that hoe could be."

"So, which one are we going to handle first?" I looked at him for direction.

Mayhem was almost always level-headed, so I always looked to him for guidance on most shit.

"First, I think it's time that we get our families and shit down to the safe house until this shit is handled. I got a wife and kids now, Frank. I gotta move differently and strategically."

"We ain't no fucking pussies, nigga. We gotta keep them here! I don't want shit happening to my nieces and nephews down in Arkansas and we here in Chicago. The best thing we can do for them is to keep moving how we been moving but beef up security. Not none of our workers but real deal secret service type security."

"I guess that makes sense. Does this mean that we are going to have to tell everyone who you really are?"

"Nah, not yet. I don't trust nobody no more besides you. I'm glad I never told Alex shit about me. Look how this bitch did me, bruh. I took care of that hoe. Financed that hoe. Kept her in the nicest cars and clothes," I vented.

"Taiwan?" he questioned me.

I shrugged my shoulders in response to that, because I didn't know. She was going to have to prove herself to me, man. How I know she wasn't trying to use me for something?

"Don't make her pay for something she hasn't done to you yet. Understand?"

Ignoring what he said, "I need a fucking blunt, mane! Five mothafuckin' years, man. Five! Five, nigga! Ooowweee, I'mma kill that hoe," I snapped.

"Aye, let's go to my cave, and I'mma get you that gas," Mayhem said.

Mayhem got up and then held his hand out to help me up. "And call the tow truck to get that shit from in front of my house. You messing up my aesthetics," Mayhem said and laughed.

If I didn't have nobody else in this cruel ass world, I knew that I had my brother from another mother.

TAIWAN

I had been upstairs in the room, sitting in the middle of the bed for like twenty minutes. I was supposed to have showered and went back downstairs to talk to Olena about everything that's been going on, but I have been sitting up here shaking. I ain't never in my life been in a shootout, and I didn't expect my first one to be days after I turned thirty. Frank had no qualms about locking people up to get what he wanted or even killing people. Frank was a fucking ruthless ass murderer, and he didn't even care, and I was a fucking accomplice. I get the reason why he killed the two men that were shooting at us, but he didn't have to drag the man out of the truck and kill him. He could have just let him die on his own. The man was a bloodied mess.

Knock! Knock!

"Tai, I'm coming in," Olena said and pushed the door in a little.

Olena walked in holding a sleeping Pier and sat at the foot of the bed.

"What's wrong, bae? I don't like seeing you like this. You came in and rushed up here. Did the lunch date go bad?"

"Frank is a killer, Olena. Like a legit killer. Like I saw it with my own two eyes."

"But you knew that though. You didn't think Mayhem was laying niggas down and Frank wasn't, right? Even Malice has a couple of bodies under him. That's something that you just have to deal with, or not at all. I will tell you this, Frank will not hurt you unless you hurt him. He's a sweetheart," Olena pleaded his case.

"He locked me in a room, Olena," I whispered as if someone else was in the room.

"What kind of room?" she asked.

"A fucking box. It was cold. He played loud music and flashing lights. It would make a mothafucka go crazy if you sat in there long enough. It's how he tortures people."

By the look on Olena's face, she didn't know anything I was talking about.

"Frank snatched me up by my hair, dragged me down the stairs, and threw me in there like I was a piece of trash after Alex shot him. That's where I was. That's why I naked and bloody," I admitted.

"Wait a minute. Frank… what? I'm so confused right now. If he did all of that, then why on earth are you bouncing around the city with him?"

"It's something inside of him that I want to unlock. The loving part of him. Frank is bottled up and full of rage, and I wish I knew why. What has Mayhem told you about him?"

"Surprisingly, nothing at fucking all. His and Frank's friendship is rock solid. I know nothing about Frank but what I can see and what he's told me out of his own mouth. Mayhem tells me everything, but he doesn't talk about Frank. The most he's ever told me was that Frank ain't have a normal childhood."

"See!" I hissed. "That. I want to know what his childhood was like. I want to know why he thinks locking people in boxes is normal. Olena, I can see myself falling in love with him, but I know after what Alex did to him, he'll never trust another woman a day in his life. I'm afraid I won't ever know what real love is like. Romero is going to kill me. He had someone shoot at us earlier, and that's why I can't stop fucking shaking, Olena. I never had that happen before. I just want to get under these covers and never come out." I started crying.

Olena patted my thigh. "Taiwan, the best decision you could have ever made was leaving Italy. That man could not give you what the fuck you deserved, and you know that. You deserved to be shown off. Look at this banging ass body. This juicy ass and juicy tits. Everything will be fine. I can promise you that. Also, maybe you and Frank don't need to rush into anything until all of this shit blows over and he gets help for his childhood struggles," Olena advised.

"You're right. I'll talk to him about it later. Right now, I think I just need a nap or something."

"Take a nap, and I'll be downstairs when you wake up."

She hugged me and walked out of the room with Pier. I thought that I was going to take a nap, but I found myself staring at the ceiling. An hour later, I was still staring at the ceiling when the door opened, and Frank swaggered into the room. He had a new hat on his head, flipped to the back, and he stood over the bed. His eyes were bloodshot red with little bags under them, which meant that he was high as a kite.

"Frank..." I called his name and paused when he ran his thick, pink tongue across his juicy bottom lip.

"What's up, mama?" he whispered.

"Can we talk about something?"

He didn't reply, but he held his hand out for me to take it. I gripped it and sat up in the bed. He then pulled me to my feet, and I couldn't help but to stare at him. Even in his high state, he was handsome. It was something about him wearing his hat to the back that turned me on. Why did something so simple as him wearing his hat to the back make me want to drop my shorts for him?

"Wh-what-why are you staring at me like that?" I choked out.

"You sexy as fuck, ma. I like looking at your brown ass," he said and laughed.

My hands were balled into tight fists, shaking at my sides, and Frank noticed it. He used his big masculine hands to grip mine. He brought them up to his big, pink lips and placed small, wet kisses on them both.

"I know you scared and shit, but..." He paused as if he was trying to find the right words to say. He took a deep breath. "I'm not going to promise that you won't be in any more shootouts, especially with that cocker spaniel on the loose. Once all this shit is over with, we are going to work on us being together. You still my baby mama though," he said and kissed my fists again.

"About that..." I paused and tried to slip my fists out of his, but he didn't let go.

"About what, Tai?"

"I think that we shouldn't rush into anything until you get over Alex and talk to me about your childhood. I won't get into another relationship with another person that I don't know," I whispered.

Ignoring me, Frank walked me into the bathroom. The moment we were in the bathroom, he turned me around so that we were looking at each other in the mirror. I could feel his heart beating a mile a minute as if he was scared, but of what? What was so damning about his childhood that he would be scared to talk about it with me... with anyone besides Mayhem.

"You're scared, Frank," I whispered as tears sprang into my eyes, and I didn't even know why.

He gave me a simple nod. A part of me wanted to force him to talk about it, but I thought against it. I didn't want anything with us to be forced. I wanted him to feel comfortable enough to talk to me about it. He reached into his pocket and pulled his phone out and set it on the sink in front of me. He went into the time clock app and set a timer for fifteen minutes. I looked up at him, and he closed his eyes and took a deep breath.

"Fifteen minutes, Tai. I'm going to give you fifteen minutes to ask me whatever it is you want to ask me. Anything. I'm going to answer it truthfully, and after that, we are not going to talk about it anymore."

"That's not fair. I need more than fifteen minutes." I huffed.

"Fifteen minutes can easily go to no minutes. I'm giving you a chance," he said while his hand was hovering over the start button.

I don't even know what to ask because I knew nothing about him, and I didn't want to ask shit like his birthday or nothing like that. I wanted to know the serious shit.

"Shall I start?" he asked me.

"Ugh, sure!" I sighed.

The minute he pressed the start button, I fired off.

"Where were you born?"

"Memphis."

"Are your parents alive?"

"Far as I know, yes."

"What are their names?"

"I don't know."

I paused the timer and stared at him. "You said truthfully, Frank!" I hissed.

Reaching around me, he pressed the start button again, and said, "That was the truth."

"How do you know if your parents are alive but don't know their names? Were you adopted?"

"No."

If he wasn't adopted, why he doesn't know his parents' names? I thought to myself.

"You're wasting time."

"Grrrrrr. I don't know how to phrase this next question." I pouted.

"That's not my problem."

"Why don't you know your parents' names?"

"They gave me fake names."

Huh? This is frustrating.

"Why would your parents give you fake names?"

"Good question. When I find out, I'll let you know."

I paused the timer again and started jumping up and down out of frustration. "Frank, this is not fair. I need elaboration! AHHH!" I screamed out of frustration.

"No, you don't. You just need to ask the right questions. Try... again," he said, reaching around me and pressing the start button. I noticed that I had thirteen minutes left.

"Umm... ummm... ummm... do you have any siblings?"

He chuckled. "Just when you get hot, you get cold. Far as I know, no."

"Why don't you know anything about your life, Frank?"

He looked from side to side as if he was confused. "I don't understand the question. I'm answering your questions."

"You don't know if you have siblings. You don't know your parents' names. You weren't adopted. You barely know if your parents are alive, and they gave you, their whole child, fake names. You would think your parents were government spies or something," I said.

I watched his facial expression change, and my eyes grew large. I paused the timer and turned around to look up at him. "Frank?" I called his name and searched his face for answers.

"Ask me a question," he said. He reached over me and started the timer again.

Leaning in closer to him, I whispered, "Your parents were spies?"

"Yes."

"Are you a spy?"

"No."

I felt like I was on to something and was getting happy that I had ten minutes left to ask him questions. "Is your real name Frank?"

"No."

"What is it?"

"What is what?"

"What is your real name? Gosh, don't be smart."

"Chaz Bourne."

"How long have you gone by Frank?"

"Since I was fourteen."

"Your parents put you in that torture box?"

"No."

"Who put you in the torture box?"

"Rickey."

"Who is Rickey?"

"A nobody. He's dead."

"Did Alex know this information?"

"No."

"Do you miss your parents?"

"No. I'm thirty-six. Haven't seen them since they dropped me off at the airport on my fourteenth birthday."

"Wow... Um... Do you have old friends... like from Memphis?"

"My only friend is Mayhem."

"Do you know your parents' location?"

"No."

"So how you know they are alive?"

"They send me a postcard once a year in Morse code."

"So, you communicate with your parents once a year?"

"No, they communicate with me."

"Would you like to see them again?"

"No."

"Why?"

"I just don't."

Switching subjects, I asked, "Do you care if you die?"

"No."

"Why don't you care if you die?"

"We all have to die someday anyway. Don't have much to live for anyway."

I looked into his eyes, and he wasn't lying. I was getting even sadder the more I stared into them.

"Do you have thoughts of suicide?"

"Often."

"Frank..." I whispered as tears pooled into my eyes.

With a stern look on his face, he spoke, "You're wasting time."

"You ever thought about therapy?"

"No."

"Who do you care about, Frank?"

"The Baileys."

"Why would you want to kill yourself if you have a whole family who cares about you?"

"I'm a burden sometimes."

"Do you enjoy killing?"

"Yes."

"Why do you enjoy killing?"

"The one thing that brings me complete satisfaction."

"How many kids do you want to have?"

"I'm okay with one."

"What made you get a dick piercing?"

"Alex."

"Do you still love, Alex?"

"Yes."

You can't get mad about that, Tai. They were together for years, I thought to myself.

"Can you see yourself being married?"

"Not anymore."

"Can you see yourself loving—**beep, beep, beep**— me?" I whispered.

"Well, that's the end of that," Frank said, but it wasn't the end for me.

After that intense round of questioning, I felt like I knew everything about him, but nothing at all. I needed elaboration on most of those questions. I needed to know why he felt like he was a burden. I wanted to know why he got satisfaction from killing people. I wanted to know why he felt like he didn't have much to live for. He has a whole damn family that cares about him and his wellbeing. He's been a Bailey longer than he was Chaz Bourne, and he thinks about killing himself daily. That was why Frank was so damn reckless with everything he did. Was it crazy that I felt more connected to him than ever?

Frank gripped my face and used his big thumbs to swipe at the tears that had slipped down my eyes. He licked his lips before placing his thick lips on mine. He continued to hold my face while he gave me a kiss that was making me weak in my knees. Frank pushed his tongue into my mouth, and I happily accepted it. I rested my hands on his waist while we continued to tongue wrestle. When he finally pulled back, we stared at each other some more before Frank grabbed at the bottom of my t-shirt.

"Frank, maybe we should—" I started.

"Shhhh."

He lifted my shirt above my head and threw it across the bathroom. He reached around me and unhooked my bra, and it slowly fell to the floor. My titties fell a little, but my nipples weren't pointing to the ground. Frank stared at me for so long that I covered them out of embarrassment.

"Don't do that, ma," Frank spoke lowly. "I just get caught up in looking at you for some odd reason. You are beautiful as hell, Taiwan. Seeing you cry twice in one day is really just fucking with me. You really fuck with me, huh?"

I nodded my head slowly.

"I fucks with that, Tai, but come on out these shorts though."

"I still have the shoot-out all over me," I whispered.

Frank ignored me and put his fingers in my waistband and pulled my shorts down. I kicked out of them, and he picked me up and set me on the cold ass sink. He laid me back until the back of my head was touching the mirror. He gripped my ankles and spread my legs wide open. My pussy was already drenched.

"You forgot to ask me one question."

"Yeah?"

"If I liked to eat pussy."

I opened my mouth to ask him, but Frank had already started kissing up my thigh until he got to my pussy. He ran his tongue up and down my pussy slowly, and it felt amazing. I used my hand to spread my fat pussy lips open so that he could focus on my clit.

"Move 'em. She gonna come out when she ready for me," Frank said.

Frank dipped his tongue inside of my hole, and my whole body went warm. He swirled his thick tongue around inside as if he was looking for something. I could feel my clit swelling as I got more and more turned on.

"See, there she goes," Frank whispered before attacking my clit.

"My Goddddd."

"Mmmhh."

"Frannnkkkk, I'm cumming," I moaned.

Frank let off my clit just to stick his tongue back in my hole to catch every drop of me. After that, he went right back to my clit as if my pussy wasn't about to give out. If Frank didn't have my ankles, I would have bounced off this damn sink. Frank was licking and sucking on my clit, not caring that I was on the verge of having my second orgasm back to back. I started bucking against his face, and he loved it, and it excited him even more. I was bucking so hard that I knocked the hat off his head, and I had started rubbing his waves backward. My body started to convulse extremely hard, and the butterflies in my lower stomach were doing the most.

"Frank!" I screamed.

"Mmmhhuh."

"Frank!" I screamed even louder.

I started squirting, and this nigga didn't even move. He kept eating until my body went limp against the sink. My heart was beating so fast that it felt like I was about to have a heart attack. I watched as Frank unbuttoned his pants and pushed them and his briefs into the middle of his thighs. He started stroking his dick, and the pre-cum oozed from the head, making me lick my lips.

"Come here," he whispered.

I hopped off the sink and almost fell because my knees were weak from fucking with him. He turned me around so that I was facing the mirror. I had to lean over on the sink to hold myself up. That last orgasm took me clean out.

Frank wrapped his big comfortable arm around my waist. "Don't worry, boo. I'll hold you up."

He tapped the head of his dick on my already overly sensitive clit, making me groan. He dipped his knees and eased his way inside of me.

"Ooo shit," he mumbled. "It's real slippery up in here. Spread that ass open; I want to go deeper."

After doing as I was told, he thrust deeper inside of me. Once I felt that metal on my spot, my mouth fell into an 'o' shape. I looked at him in the mirror, and his face wore the same expression that I was making. Frank started circling his hips, and each time he centered, I felt his piercing tap on my G-spot.

"Babyyy," I groaned, getting ready to tap out on him.

"I know… I know. I feel you tightening up around me. I'm about to bust one with you."

I could feel Frank's dick pulsating against my walls. I felt every drop of his semen as he sprayed my walls. We stayed connected until his dick got soft, and he eased out of me. He didn't say anything to me, but we continued to stare at each other. After a few moments of being lost in each other's eyes, he finally broke eye contact and started the shower for us.

Later that night. 2:00 A.M.

I had been up since Frank and I retired to Mayhem's guest house. No matter how many orgasms he gave me earlier, I still couldn't sleep. I tried reading, but I couldn't focus on it. My mind was on everything Frank told me earlier. He told me that he often thought about killing himself, and that just didn't sit right with me. I wanted to be able to love him through all of that, but I felt like after what Alex did to him, he would never get close to another woman, even if it were me. He would probably care for me deeply but actually fall in love with me, no.

The moon was shining bright, so the room was lit up. Looking over at Frank, I could tell that he had a lot on his mind, even in his sleep. He probably wasn't even sleeping well. The covers were at his waist with some of the hair from his pubes sticking out. I never found pubic hair sexy, but Frank had his low. His chest was slowly rising and falling. There was a light coat of sweat covering his body, and it shouldn't have been, because this room was cold as fuck. Frank turned the air down to fifty degrees. After we finished another round of sex, this nigga was sweaty as fuck, and I was shivering. I had to find one of my sweaters to put on with a pair of leggings to keep warm. Frank's left hand was resting on his rock hard abs, and his right arm was resting across his eyes. The tightness of his forehead and his fist being balled up was what worried me. His forehead was so tight that I could see the veins in it. He must have been having a bad dream.

I grabbed my phone to text Olena to see if she was up. I really needed to talk to someone who understood Frank more than I did.

Me: *Lee, you up.*
Olena: *Always. The twins are in here sleeping wild.*
Me: *I need to talk to Mayhem... about Frank. When will he not be busy?*
Olena: *He's in the kitchen right now feeding Pier.*
Me: *Okay. Thanks, bestie.*
Olena: *You're welcome, and Tai... just give Frank some time. He really really loved Alex. Like, he would have died for her skank ass if he needed to. She was his first love and had never been in love before. Just give him some time. Love you.* 😊
Me: *Love you, back.*

I put my phone back down on the nightstand and slowly climbed out of bed. I looked at Frank again, and he was still in the same spot. I slid on my house shoes and walked out of the guesthouse.

"Whew, yes, Lord!" I whispered to myself because the night air felt better than inside of that guesthouse. I could feel my bones warming up.

Once I was closer to the kitchen, I noticed that the door was slightly ajar. I assumed that Olena had already told Mayhem that I was coming to talk to him. I eased in the door, and he was sitting at the table with his phone propped up, watching something. He was holding Pier against his chest, burping him. Fatherhood really looked good on Mayhem. As soon as I took a seat at the table, the tears started forming in my eyes.

"Sis, why you up in here crying this late? What he did?" Mayhem asked.

Mayhem paused his phone and put it in his pocket.

"He didn't do anything. I'm just afraid for him. For you. This whole situation. Earlier, we talked... and it scared me, Mayhem. Frank told me that he often thought about suicide and that he felt like he was a burden to you, even though he loves your family."

Mayhem's eyebrow went up, and he stood up. "He said that to you? Said that he was a burden to me? He said that tonight? To you?"

"Yes. He gave me fifteen minutes to ask him anything that I wanted to ask him, and I found out *everything*. Took a minute, but I did. I felt helpless. He still loves Alex, and I asked him if he could see himself loving me, and he didn't answer the question. Mayhem, I want to love Frank through all of this. I want him to know that I'm not with him for his money or any of that. I have my own."

Clearly, Mayhem was pissed. Maybe I shouldn't have said that Frank felt suicidal and that he felt like he was a burden to him. His face was turning a different shade of red. He eased back in his seat and sighed. He closed his eyes for a few moments and then opened them again.

"Taiwan, Frank is different. He's lived a hard life, and trust me, you must give him some time, but if he shared something with you that he's never shared with anyone else, he's definitely feeling you. Sis, this nigga is about to kill the head of a cartel for you. What more do you want from him?"

"What more do I want from him? I want him to be comfortable living the life that he has. I want him to not think about taking his life! I want him to not love Alex! I want him to love me! I can give him everything that she didn't. I can give him real love! A love that he has never experienced before!" I stressed through my tears.

"Tai, sweetheart, calm down. Frank knows that you can give him all of that. He wouldn't be laid up with you if he didn't know that."

"Does he? Frank keeps everything to himself. Everything. You ask him a question and it's either *yes, no*, or *sure*. What if I give him everything that I have to give and then he starts feeling he's becoming a burden to *me*? I can't stop thinking about him killing himself. What if I fall even deeper in love with him and he does that! I would be left here, picking up the pieces, wondering what I could have done better. I'm scared, Mayhem! I am really scared."

I placed my head in hand and sobbed.

"I'm scared too, Taiwan."

I whipped my head around toward the door, and Frank was standing there with his hands in his basketball shorts, still shirtless. His eyes were unreadable, and I wasn't sure if he was angry or not.

Mayhem stood and walked toward the entry of the kitchen. "Frank, you and I will have a conversation. Goodnight, you two," Mayhem said and walked out of the kitchen.

"Come here, shorty," Frank said in such a flat tone.

I stood up and walked slowly toward him. "Frank, please don't be…" I said and paused before he grabbed me and pulled me into his chest.

"I'm not mad. You did what you felt was right."

He grabbed my hand and led me out the door. We walked hand in hand back toward the guesthouse.

"How did you know where I was?"

"I felt you get out of bed."

"You did?"

"Yes. I pick up on a lot of small shit. I actually heard you tapping on your phone to Olena."

"How you know I was texting Olena?"

"I looked at your phone when you left. I wanted to make sure you wasn't bold enough to be texting another nigga to meet up with him after I just beat that pussy down. Fuck you mean?"

I chuckled. "So, if I…" I paused and acted if I was about to smack him, and he grabbed my wrist before my hand even got close to his face. He let me hand go, and I rubbed where he grabbed my wrist. "Wow. You're quick."

"I know. Don't do it—"

I cut him off by trying to smack him again, but he grabbed my wrist again and spun me around so that I was facing him. I was walking backward and looking up at him.

"What I just tell you, woman?"

"Just need to make sure that you are on point."

"You ain't got to ever worry about me not being on point."

Once we were in the guesthouse, he told me to get undressed, and so did he. We got in bed, and he pulled me on top of him, and I nuzzled in his neck. I instantly felt warm in that cold ass room. He wrapped his arms around me, and my skin grew even hotter. After a moment of silence, he started speaking.

"Taiwan, I'm fine, bae. I promise. We are going to be straight. Don't worry to much because I don't want no wrinkles in that pretty brown skin. Get some sleep."

"We are going to sleep like this?"

"Yes. Things like this makes you happy. If it makes you happy, then I'll do it."

"I don't want you to sacrifice your—"

"Sssshhhh. This won't be no every night thing. Go to sleep."

He started sliding his hands up and down my back, and before long, I was knocked out.

RUBEE

THE NEXT DAY

Today was not my day, so I had been in bed for majority of the day. Raylee was upset that she had to stay in my room and play with her toys. The only time I got out of the bed was to feed her, and that was this morning and this afternoon. I'm sure she was hungry again because it was now five in the evening, but she hadn't said anything. I don't know if I was upset at myself for not seeing the signs or upset for my daughter, who's going to grow up without a father. My cousin never did hit me back up with the information I asked him to look at, but he didn't have to, because when I came home from Kade's house, Bash had left me note. I picked the note up off my nightstand and read it again.

Rubee,

By now, you probably already know what's going on. I fucked up. Made some stupid ass decisions, so I gotta get low. Please don't let this shit make you think that I never loved you or our daughter. If I ain't done shit else in my life, just know that Raylee is one of the best things that could have ever happened to me. She's my pride and joy, and I'll forever think about her and you until I take my last breath. I wasn't truthful in the beginning, Rube. Meeting you wasn't an accident, but falling in love with you damn sure was. I wasn't supposed to do that. It's just that I couldn't leave Alex out in the cold when she been holding me down for the last fifteen years. I was supposed to leave the night I packed that bag before all of this shit went left but looking at my lil twin fucked all of that up. Listen, promise me that you won't tell Raylee bad things about me. Promise me. I did my best to be a good father to her. I'm sorry. I emptied my savings and over half of my checking into her trust fund, and it should be at least eighty thousand dollars in there. Take care of yourself and my daughter, Rubee.

Bash.

After reading it for the thousandth time today, I felt a queasiness in my stomach. My mouth began to water. I jumped out of the bed and went into the bathroom. I dry-heaved about five times before something eventually came up. I hadn't eaten at all today, so I didn't even know how something came out. After washing my mouth out, I climbed back in the bed. My eyes became so heavy that I eventually fell asleep.

An hour later...

I was being violently shaken. My eyes popped open, and I was staring up at Kade Lewis, who was now holding Raylee in his arms.

"The hell yo' problem is?" he snapped.

"Kade..." I whispered.

Snatching the note off the nightstand, he started waving it around in my face. "Is this what you mad about, huh? Is this why you got your daughter downstairs standing on the counter trying to find you some food to make you because you don't feel good? Is this what you don't feel good about?"

"Kade, please stop screaming at me!" I shouted.

"I ain't screaming yet, Rubee. Just because that dude is a goofy, you can't stop being a damn mama. You ain't fed your daughter since earlier."

"How you know?"

"When she opened the door for me—"

"RAYLEE! YOU OPENED THE DOOR FOR A STRANGER?"

Raylee started crying, and I instantly felt bad. I never wanted to make my baby cry like that.

"Raylee, let me talk to your mother for a second. Go into your room and play, and I'll come get you in just a moment, okay," Kade said before kissing her small wet cheek and letting her down.

When she skated out of the room, Kade closed and locked the door. He walked over to me and snatched the covers back and pulled them off the bed. I didn't have nothing but my sleeping dress from Victoria's Secret on. He gripped my neck and pulled me up from the bed to my feet. The grip he had on my neck, forced me to look at him.

"Again, I'mma ask you what the fuck ya problem is? You shouting at Ray when she ain't done shit to you. I been calling your black ass all fucking day, and you been ignoring me. I called you, and Raylee answered the phone and said that you were sad and sleepy, so you couldn't come to the phone. She told me that she was going to the kitchen to fix you something to eat and that she would call me back. I sped over here so baby girl wouldn't burn the house down while your dumb ass was up here sleep. She asked me who it was before climbing in the window to see if it was really me before opening the door for me, so you hollered at her for no fucking reason, and you better not ever do that shit again. You understand me?"

"That's *my* daughter, Kade! You don't—"

The way he raised his eyebrow told me that I shouldn't say another word, and I pressed my lips together tightly.

"What did I say? I'mma be helping you raise her when you get your fucking mind right, because Bash ain't coming back. It's over with for that nigga!"

"He's Rubee's father."

"So, that's why you sick, huh? That's why you sick. You been fucking with me heavy for a lil' minute, but ya baby daddy do you

AN INSANE LOVE 3

wrong and leave you and your daughter, but you crying for him. You made your choice. I'm out," Kade said and let my neck go.

I didn't say anything until he approached the door. "Kade, don't go. Please, you have to understand."

"I ain't gotta understand shit. I'm good on you, Rubee. When I leave, don't call my phone or nothing. How dare you run a bitch away from my house, but you crying because this nigga about to get that work when ya cousin and Frank catch him. That's his own damn fault. The nigga used you... straight used you, and you looking me in my face about to cry over him again."

"Ka-ka-ka..." I tried to say his name until I felt the vile coming up in my throat again. I rushed into the bathroom and threw up again.

While I was puking my guts up, I heard the bedroom door slam. I washed my mouth again and then washed my face. I stared at myself in the mirror for a minute. I was crying because my feelings were hurt. I liked Kade a lot. A whole lot, but it still didn't compare to finding out via a letter that you were most likely going to never see your baby daddy again. As much as I hated Bash for being a fuck nigga, I was still hurting for my daughter because she was smart. She was going to be asking about her father, and what was I supposed to say? Was I supposed to tell her that her daddy left us to probably go be with the girl that he's known for fifteen years? How could I explain to my daughter that she was never going to see him again? Raylee was smart and would continue to ask questions. I stared at myself for a few more minutes before I put on my house shoes and walked out of the room.

I walked to Raylee's door and then pushed it open, but she wasn't in there. I went to the top of the stairs, and I smelled food. I rushed down the stairs and saw Kade standing at the island, cutting up chicken and vegetables, while Raylee was sitting on the island with a vegetable in front of her, and she was cutting it up with a knife in her hand.

"Mama, Kade is letting me help him cut up the veggies. I'm doing it right, Kadey?" Raylee asked him.

"That's a knife!" I spoke to Kade through a tight-lipped smile. "Yes, you are doing it right, babe."

"It is, Rubee," he said without even looking at me. He looked up at Raylee who was cutting her vegetable slowly but surely. "Baby girl, what is a knife?"

"Something you use to cut food."

"Anddddd?"

"It's sharp."

"Annd?"

"You walk with the cutting part toward the ground, and... oh, don't ever run with it because you can fall and cut your intes... intest..."

"Intestines, baby girl."

"Right. You can fall and cut your intestines out. I can only use a knife with my mom's or your permission."

"See. She's fine," Kade said to me.

He still was not looking at me, and it was bothering me. After Rubee was finished cutting her vegetables, he picked her up so she could put the knife in the sink. Just like he told her, Raylee was carrying the knife with the sharp part down. He had his arm wrapped around her little belly and his other arm under her legs. She picked up her vegetables and emptied them into the pot, and Kade put her down on her feet, and she went hopped in her seat at the bar and picked up her crayons.

"You should feel better soon, Mommy," Raylee said to me.

What did I do to have such a perfect daughter, whose world was about to be turned upside down? Kade placed what was on his chopping board into the pot. I looked into the pot and saw that he was making me homemade chicken noodle soup. When he walked by me, I tried to grab him, but he moved my hands and went and sat at the bar next to Raylee.

"Kade, can I see you please? In the other room."

He ignored me and kept looking at Raylee color. Fuck him. I wasn't going to beg him to talk to me anymore. If he wanted to be a bitch, then I could be a bitch too. I sat at the kitchen table and watched him and Raylee interact, and it was the cutest thing. Forty-five minutes later, Kade got up and grabbed two plates out of the cabinet. He fixed Raylee a plate, and then he fixed mine.

"You gonna eat?" I asked him, expecting him not to answer.

"Nah, I have things to do. I left work to come here. Just be at work in the morning."

"You can dress yourself." I huffed. "You just want to torture me, Kade. I'm not with that. I won't be ignored in your home."

"You'll be working. See you tomorrow," he said to me before he disappeared out of the kitchen, and I heard him slam the front door.

"Is he mad at you?" Raylee asked.

"No. No, honey. He's not mad. Concerned… worried."

"My dad slams things when he's mad."

"I know. Finish eating."

After we finished eating, I took her upstairs so I could put her in the bath. I know I'm going to be good living here alone, because I was always here alone, but to know that I would never see him again, still hurt a little.

Raylee was in the tub playing with her toys, so I called Mayhem, and he picked up on the first ring.

"What up, cuz? My bad for not getting back to you yesterday, but a lot of shit going on, but that nigga Bash is living foul, and that nigga gone, Rubee. Get ya tears out the way now. I'm telling you."

"He left me a note."

"I bet he did. That nigga is a snake. He was working with Kharisma. Him and Alex been together for years."

"I know," I whispered. "Are you talking about *your* Kharisma?"

"She ain't *my* shit, but yeah. Her hoe ass. She gone too. Wait, why you sounding like this? Sounding like ya nose is stopped up and shit. You been crying?"

"Nah, well, yeah, but I think I kind of lost Kade. He came over, and I was a little sad that *she* is never going to see *him* again. Like, can you give her a chance to say goodbye to him?"

"You pushing it, cuz, but I don't know. I'll think about it. Also, don't be alarmed about the extra security that's going to be hanging around ya house. Some shit about to go down, and I got to make sure everybody straight. Love you, family," he said and hung up.

I washed Raylee up and put on her nightgown. We got in bed and watched TV for the rest of the night until we both fell asleep.

The next morning

I was running late to Kade's house, and I was sure that he was going to be pissed, but I didn't give a damn. I pulled my car up behind a white Honda Accord. The car had a paper tag on it, so it had to be brand new.

"Who the hell visiting him this early in the morning?" I whispered to myself.

I got out and got Raylee out of the car. She was still knocked out, so I had to cradle her. I started kicking on the door with boots on. Moments later, a short, light-skinned petite bitch answered the door in a little ass dress. If Kade was fucking on her, I was going to beat his and her ass once I put my baby down in the bed. This nigga had to be stupid. This bitch didn't look a day over eighteen, and he had her up in this house like she was his girl or something. My adrenaline was running through my damn body at rapid speed.

"Who the fuck is you?" I hissed.

She looked at me with her face scrunched up and then smacked her lips. "Girl, you showed up here. Who are you?"

"Tawanna, watch out," Kade said from behind the door.

He pulled the door back some more. He had a white towel wrapped around his waist and his body was soaking wet.

"Really! Really!" I shouted, waking my baby up, and she started crying.

The bitch I now knew as Tawanna was looking him and up and down and licking her lips. "I love seeing you topless, Kade."

Ignoring Tawanna, he took Raylee out of my arms, and she happily went to him. He walked away from the door, leaving me to stare in this green-eyed bitch's face.

"Can we help you?" she asked me.

Pow!

I sucker punched that bitch right in her mouth.

"Help that, hoe," I snapped before she tried to swing on me, and I dodged it.

We started fighting right there on his porch. I pushed her right off the porch and onto her back. Just as I was getting ready to climb on her and pummel her for her smart-ass mouth, I heard another woman's voice.

"What is going on out here?"

I turned to see Kalena standing at the door in a small ass dress as well.

"This crazy bitch attacked me!" Tawanna shouted.

Kade appeared back at the door, now wearing a robe. He wore an angry look on his face. It seemed like he got to me in two steps. He snatched me up and carried me in the house and into his bedroom and slammed the door.

"Where is my daughter? I'm out of here. You got another bitch up in here. You play too many fucking games for me, Kade. You come over to my house trying to pretend to be mad because I care that my daughter is not about to have a father, but you have another bitch up in here playing house. Who is she, Kade?"

While I was ranting, Kade kept rubbing his temples. He didn't say anything, and it was pissing me off even further.

"Rubee, Wanna is Kalena's friend. They drove here from college right after they left the club, hence the reason they are dressed the way they are dressed. I was in the shower when I heard you kicking on the door like you were the police… hence the reason why I had the towel on," he spoke lowly.

"Why was she talking like that then? Asking me why I was here?

She told you that she liked to see you shirtless… in my face, like I was some punk bitch."

"That's just how she is. What girl you know don't have crush on their friend's big brother? That's all. Come here, now!"

After getting close to him, he wrapped his arms around me. "Listen, you have to chill with the crazy shit, Rubee. If you don't disrespect me, I won't disrespect you. Crying over that nigga yesterday really fucked me up, because I thought that we were kind of building something. Like, I get that he was your first and he's Ray's dad, but that nigga a fraud. You don't weep for fraud ass niggas. Raylee is going to be well taken care after he's gone."

"Where is she?"

"In the guestroom, sleeping. You really need to stop shouting around her. Do you understand that?"

I nodded my head and started trying to put my hand in his robe, but he moved back.

"Nah, go get my clothes so I can get dressed. I'm already late, fooling with you and your shit this morning."

"It's been weeks."

"It's going to be even longer until you can learn how to act right. Go do your job while I grease up."

I stomped away from him and went into his closet. I wanted to pick out the ugliest shit that he had and put it together, but Kade would wear it just to piss me off. I knew how he was. By the time he put on his clothes and got in the studio to take pictures, it was a little past ten.

"You work for yourself, Kade. Why are you rushing?" I asked him, trying to keep up with his strides toward the guestroom.

"No, I do not work for myself, babe. I work for your cousin."

Once we were inside the bedroom, Kade placed a kiss on Raylee's cheek, and then placed a rough one on my forehead before heading out of the door. I was standing there stuck until he stuck his head back in the door.

"And oh, before you leave today, make sure you apologize to Wanna." My mouth fell open, and he held his hand up to stop me from speaking. "You were wrong. Lesson number one in being an adult begins today. Apologize, and I may think about sticking my finger inside of you later on."

I sighed and rolled my eyes, and he laughed before blowing me a kiss before leaving. I stood in the same spot until I heard the front door close and the alarm system go off. I hated that my lips automatically curved into a smile. I hated him, but I loved him at the same time.

Loved?

BASH

TWO DAYS AGO

I had been on edge ever since the meeting was over. This nigga put a picture of my girl in my pocket with a bounty on her head. There was nothing I could fucking do about it. I couldn't face Rubee with a bloody face, so I went to Kharisma's house, just to chill out before I came home, and to see if she talked to Alex. I'd been thinking about her like crazy since I found out that she knew about Raylee. I didn't want her to find out like that. Eventually, I was going to tell her, but shit just was too crazy, and I didn't want her to spaz and blow our cover.

After I pulled up to Kharisma's house, I knocked on the door, and she opened it with only a tank-top and some shorts on.

"Give me one reason why I shouldn't choke you right now. Why the fuck did you call me with Alex on the phone? You been trying to break us up for the longest. Fuck! I wasn't ready for her to know just yet. I was going to tell her."

"She asked me to call you, and she literally forced me to. I didn't have a choice. How long did you think that you were going to be able to hold that secret in? She was bound to find out."

"Whatever," I said and brushed by her into her house.

"What happened to you?"

"Frank."

She gasped. "He knows?"

"Nah. I spoke out of turn, and he hit me in my shit. I can't go home with my face swollen. I just want to chill out here before I go home. Rubee probably not there anyway. You know she been fucking with Kade. I know they fucked because she definitely doesn't fuck me anymore."

"Damn. I ain't heard nothing about that," she said.

"Uh huh." I sighed before walking back to the room that Alex and I used to get down in.

Moments later, Kharisma brought me an ice pack to put it on my face to help the swelling go down.

"When the last time you talk to Alex?" I asked her.

"When she hung up on me. I told her to call me when she made it to her destination, but she hasn't called yet. You think that she was caught?"

"Nah, I don't think she was."

After an awkward moment of silence, Kharisma walked out of the room and shut the door, and before long, I was out like a light.

Two hours later.

"BASH!"

I jumped awake to Kharisma screaming my name.

"What, girl? You scared me, girl."

"We have to go now! Rubee just called my phone and asked me who I was. She had to have been going through your phone bill. If she went through your phone bill, then she's going to ask Mayhem to search the number. It's going to lead back to me, and we are going to get killed. We have to go, now!"

"You are being paranoid right now. Just chill."

"Nigga, you are really underestimating who Mayhem is. Come on, we have to go! You can stay if you want, but I'm getting ready to go. I'm not about to stick around to get killed. That nigga is going to have to work to kill me. Bye," she said and vanished from the door.

She sounded serious, and she did know Mayhem just a tad bit better than I did, so I jumped up and followed her outside. She was hooking Price up in his car seat. After I jumped in the passenger seat, I pulled my phone out, and I didn't have a message or nothing. Kharisma jumped in the front seat and pulled out of the yard like a mad woman.

"Aye, take me by the house right quick so I can at least leave Rubee a note," I stressed. "I wanted her to know that I love her and Raylee, and I'm really not a bad person."

"Shut the fuck up, Bash, because yes you are. We have no time for that."

"Please. Just do me this solid. Five minutes tops. If I'm not out the house, then leave me."

She drove to my house, and I rushed inside, thankful that Rubee wasn't there. I found the first piece of paper and pen I could find. I let her know that despite the circumstances, I did love her, and my daughter is my greatest accomplishment as a man. I begged her not to speak ill of me because I did love them, shit just crazy. After I finished the letter, I found a picture of all three of us together and put it in my wallet. I walked out of the house, and Kharisma was twisting her head around as if her head was on a swivel. As soon as I put my damn foot in the door, she pulled off. I watched my house in the rearview mirror until I couldn't see it anymore. I was definitely going to miss that mothafucka.

We weren't heading toward O'Hare nor Midway airports, so I didn't know where we were going.

"Where are we going?" I asked her. "Are you going to warn your brothers that Mayhem is after you?"

"About to drop Price off with his father, and I haven't talked to them in years, and Mayhem knows that we ain't close, so he's probably not going to fuck with them. He's not as heartless as Frank."

"I thought you ain't know who your baby daddy was?"

"I never told you that. You assumed that, so I never said anything."

We pulled up to a gate, and she stopped at the security thing and flashed them some of type of tag, and they let her in. I looked at the houses, and they were huge as fuck.

"Who your baby daddy, girl?"

"Javon Racy."

"THE Javon Racy? The starting point forward for the Chicago Bulls?"

"Yeah, he was all in my inbox around the time that me and Mayhem stopped fucking around, and I met up with him and had a wild ass night. Next thing you know, I'm pregnant. I tried to pin the baby on Mayhem, but he knew something was up."

"You just about to show up with Price. This nigga is married, Kharisma," I stressed.

"He knew he was married before he fucked me unprotected. Whose fault is that?"

I shook my head as she whipped her G-Wagon in behind his Ferrari. She got out the car and opened the back door to get Price out. Now that I think about it, Price did look exactly like Javon. Spitting image of him.

"Price, Mommy loves you more than anything in this world, okay? Everything that I have ever done is for you, okay?" she said to him as if he understood.

A lump grew in my throat because I left something like that in that note for Raylee, praying that one day she forgave me for all the sins that I committed that caused me to have to leave her forever.

As soon as Kharisma hit the top of the steps, the door came open, and Javon and his wife were standing there with a surprised look on their faces. I let the window down so I could hear, because I knew that it was about to get loud.

"Kharisma, what is this!" Javon shouted.

"You know this woman, Javon? I asked you if you knew her, and you said no!" his wife screamed.

"Look, I've gotten into some trouble, and I have to go. I didn't come here to argue with either of you. You have to look after him because I don't want him going into foster care. You have the means to take care of him," she said.

She bent down and kissed Price and hugged him tightly before she walked off the porch with Javon screaming after her. The tears were streaming down her face, and she started crying even harder when Price started screaming for her. She pulled out of the driveway and sped down the street. She looked at me, but I ain't say shit.

"Despite what you may think about me, Bash, I loved my son. Giving him to his father was the hardest thing that I have ever done in my life. Please stop judging me."

I ain't say anything. We sped toward Rockford toward the airport, and the ride was quiet. Halfway there, I received a message on my phone. I opened it, and it was from Mayhem.

May: Let's meet.

"Shit, Mayhem just texted me and said, let's meet," I said to her.

"Nigga, throw that fucking phone out. That nigga is tracking us right now."

Doing as I was told, I threw the phone out of the window.

"What about your phone?" I asked her.

"I have always had two phones. The other one is already gone," she said.

At the airport, she grabbed her purse, and we rushed to the counter to purchase two tickets to Hawaii.

"What are you names?" the lady asked.

"Ma'am, we are trying to get away from my ex-husband. He will be able to track us down if we use our real names. That's why I have this cash. Please, can you get us tickets in your name? Please," Kharisma pleaded. "He's crazy and tried to kill me already today. That's why we look like this. My current husband already fought him."

She was able to sell it because she cried the whole way to the airport, and my face was still semi swollen because of Frank hitting me in my face at the meeting.

"Okay, ma'am! Okay! We are going to get everything worked out for you two. You two are in luck because we have a semi-full flight that's about to get ready to board in about thirty minutes... I just put you two on it. I'm going to make sure that they wait on you."

Kharisma tried to hand her the cash, but she waved it off and told her to save it because she was going to need it. We rushed inside the airport, and after we went through TSA, we found our terminal, and they had just started to board. Thirty minutes later, we were sitting in our seats on our way to Hawaii. The flight was quiet, and we both had a lot on our minds. I'm sure that we both were thinking about our children that we just left behind.

After the long, uncomfortable plane ride, we were getting off the plane.

We went outside and found a cab to the hotel that I had set Alex up in. I prayed that she would be happy to see me, because I would damn sure be happy to know that she was safe.

One hour later.

We arrived at the hotel that she was staying at, and it was beautiful here. It was right on the beach, and I couldn't wait to take a dip in the pretty blue water. I went to the front and got my key from the lady. Kharisma and I went up to the room, and I let us in and let the door close softly. Walking further into the room, Alex was laid in the bed, naked, and my dick instantly rocked up. I went and sat in front of her and rubbed her hair out of her face. Her eyes fluttered open, and she let out a scream.

"Alex! Chill!"

"Bash," she said and pulled the covers up over her body. "What are you doing here? When did you get here?"

"Just a few minutes ago. Shit really bad."

She looked past me and saw Kharisma and rolled her eyes. "Where is Price and..." she said and paused. "Your daughter... with Rubee, Bash!"

She got out of the bed and started beating on me, and her fists were hurting me like crazy, but I let her do it. I knew that she was pissed.

"How could you, Bash!" She cried. "You would have never come here if shit didn't go bad! You would have stayed there and left me high and dry here."

"Alex, I love you! I love you! I never stopped. Please calm down so we can talk, please," I begged her.

She collapsed in my arms and cried. I just held her because nothing I said was going to make her feel better at the moment.

Present day

For the last couple of days, Alex ain't been talking to me, but she has been letting me eat her pussy. I'd do anything to get back in her good graces at this point. She wasn't talking to Kharisma either. I put her room on my bill, because she didn't want to sleep in the room with us. I could get used to living in Hawaii, but shit was expensive as hell here.

Today was a semi good day because I went out and caught some sun. I had a tan like crazy, but I liked it. I say it was a semi good day because Alex actually smiled at me when I came in from the beach this afternoon. We were making progress. After I got out the shower, I sat on the bed while she was laying in it. She hadn't moved from that spot since I'd been here but to shower and eat. Hopefully, I'd be able to get her to go to the beach tonight because it was pretty as hell at night.

"Do you have a picture of her?" Alex whispered.

I whipped my head around and looked at her. "Say what?"

"You heard me."

I did hear her, but I wanted to hear her say it again. I went in my wallet and pulled out the only picture that I had of her. I handed her the picture, and she stared at her for a little while before she silently started to cry.

"Alex…" I whispered her name and grabbed her foot, but she moved it back.

"I'm fine. What's she like?"

I smiled. "Raylee James is perfect. She's really smart and loves to color. She can hold a conversation with you like she's an adult. That's my side-kick, and I love her more than anything on this earth. Alex, I don't regret my daughter at all. I do regret hurting you because you deserved none of this. I'm sorry for hurting you and dragging you into this mess. You didn't ask for this shit. I should have listened to you when you said that we should leave the first year in. I became addicted to the hustle, when I should have listened to you. It probably wouldn't have been as hard to leave."

"Thank you, Bash. I needed to hear that," she replied and handed the picture back to me.

I found one of her favorite reality TV shows on, and I cuddled up behind her and watched it with her.

KADE

After work, I headed toward my house. I called that big head ass girl, and she didn't answer the phone, which infuriated me. I couldn't believe that she had me crazy like this. I wondered if she'd left my house, so I called Kalena, and she answered on the first ring.

"Ugh, you get ya first piece of good pussy, now I don't even see you anymore. Did you forget that you have a sister, honestly?" Kam said into the phone.

I chuckled. "It ain't nothing like that, sis. I promise it's not. A lot of shit is going on, and I just want to make sure—"

"Yeah, yeah, yeah, Kalena is over here with Wanna. She told me that Rubee beat her ass this morning."

"You know she a lil' off in the head. Very overprotective."

"Uh huh. Make your way over here to see me sometime soon. Damn. Here go Lena."

"Yeah, big head?" Kalena said into the phone.

"Did Rubee and Raylee leave my house?"

"They hadn't left when I left about two hours ago."

"Aight," I said and hung up the phone.

I tried to call her again, and she still didn't answer the phone.

AN INSANE LOVE 3

Twenty minutes later, I pulled in next to Maddison's car. I hoped that they didn't get to fighting and Rubee had her locked up in the house somewhere. I got out the car and walked in the house. Everything was still intact, so a fight hadn't happened. I walked around to the kitchen, and Raylee was sitting at the kitchen table with headphones on with her head in a coloring book, while Maddison was sitting at one end with a scared look on her face, and Rubee was sitting at the other end of the table, with a smug look on her face.

Ignoring the big butcher knife in the middle of the table, I asked Rubee, "What is going on?"

"Well, Marjorie popped up over here again, and I invited her in to wait on you. Don't worry, she's not cut yet, but she's going to be if she doesn't stop fucking with me… us," Rubee hissed.

Raylee hadn't heard a thing because she kept bouncing her head while coloring.

"Kade, please tell this girl that you and I are together now, and she needs to stop popping up because y'all ain't friends no more. Y'all fucked. And you can't go from friends to fucking to friends again. It just doesn't work that way."

"Maddi, Rubee and I are working on getting together, and it doesn't help that you keep popping up over here. Is there something that you and I need to discuss?"

"Yes, but I don't want to discuss it in front of this child," she hissed, and my eyes grew large.

"You better be talking about my daughter and not trying to be funny," Rubee said as her hand inched toward the handle of the butcher knife.

"Yes. Come on. Let's go on the porch," I told Maddison.

"Kade, for real?" Rubee snapped.

I gripped Rubee's chin and placed a small kiss on her lips before pushing my tongue in her mouth and pulled back at Raylee yelling *ewww*. "Now hush. I'll be back."

I walked out of the kitchen with Maddison on my heels, until we stepped outside on the porch. We stood in front of each other for a little minute before she said something.

"So, this is it, Kade? Our friendship is ending because of this little girl and her child. You remember how you said that you wanted your first child to be your baby mama or wife's first child? What happened to that? All the shit you said back in college, you are going against right now." She huffed and stomped her foot.

"Maddison, how long has it been since I been in college? Shit changes. I've changed. Hopefully, you've changed since college. If you haven't, that is your issue. The reality of it is, we can't go back to being friends. We probably could have if you weren't being disrespectful to my lady. Now, the thought of us being anything is over with. We can be cordial, and I will never disrespect you, but we can't be friends anymore. You can't be popping up at my crib like this. Aight?"

While waiting for her answer, I stuffed my hands in my pockets and looked at the porch, trying not to make eye contact. I couldn't believe that I was doing this. Even after college, I was saying that I wanted my baby mama to have mine and her first child, but it was something about Rubee that I was drawn too. Raylee is the perfect child. She's really smart and eager to learn. I'm becoming attached to her, and I hated that because I still don't know for sure what Rubee and I are. I don't want to play any more of these games with her.

"You got it, Kade. Don't call me when that lil' girl breaks your heart," Maddison said and stomped off the porch.

I watched her get in her car, back out of my driveway, and burn rubber down the road. I sighed before I walked back in the house and into the kitchen. Rubee was still sitting at the table, but she had put the knife away, and Raylee no longer had the headphones on, but she was still coloring.

"What you tell her?" she asked me.

"I told her that we couldn't be friends anymore because she disrespected you, but I feel like..." I sighed and sat in the chair across from Raylee. "I don't know, Rubee. Are you really feeling me? Or are you hypnotized by the D?"

"What's the D?" Raylee asked.

Both me and Rubee chuckled before saying 'nothing' in unison.

"I'm really feeling you, Kade. You know that. I don't give my body to just no anybody. What you mean? You think I'm overprotective of you for no reason?"

"Yeah, you could be. You could be hooked on the D, and just don't want nobody else to get it."

"I am hooked. Very hooked. I don't want nobody else to get it. I'm just scared... Kade. So much is going on. You remember the conversation that we had in the sandwich shop? I'm not like you. I'm different from you. I'm sure you want a woman with a couple of degrees like yourself, and well put together. You don't want a hot head like me. I—"

"Where is all of this coming from?"

"Always wanting me to be calm. Wanting me to apologize for fighting."

"Rubee, being a hot head is not cool. I want you calm because the way you always thinking about stabbing people can land you in jail, away from Raylee and me. You were wrong for coming at Wanna the way you did, so that's why you needed to apologize. Baby girl, degrees don't automatically make you smart; it just means that you can pay attention and take tests. I just want you to be able to make sound decisions. Do you know how many women are locked up because they reacted before thinking? You keep a razor in your cheek for God's sake, Rubee. What if I want some top spontaneously, and you cut my wang off?"

We both chuckled at the same time before she spit the razor out of her cheek and slid it across the table to me.

"I'll do better, Kade, but I'm jealous. I was never this jealous with *you know who* but with you... I'm ready to kill anybody."

"You ain't got nothing to worry about. I promise you don't."

I reached across the table and pinched her cheek.

"Oh, I meant to tell you that I have appointments to look at Raylee's schools for Kindergarten. She's only four, but her pre-school teacher said that she would feel like she was holding her back if she kept her for another year. So, I been looking at schools, and I have an appointment with two of the best ones in the morning. My baby is not a baby anymore, Kade," she said and then looked at Ray, who was giving her the biggest smile.

"I'm coming with you," I told her.

"You don't have—"

"What I say?"

"Okay. You can tell me about them while we eat dinner, since you didn't take anything out."

"I wasn't going to stay, but when shorty pulled up, I made it my business to stay."

I shook my head and stood up. I knew a place that both her and Raylee would enjoy. Chuck E. Cheese's. I wanted to tire Raylee out because the things that I was going to do to her mom was going to damn near wake up the whole block.

That night

We stayed at Chuck E. Cheese's for three hours. Raylee wanted to play every game instead of eating, and I let her. When we finally got her to sit down, Rubee and I discussed the schools that she chose. St. Mary's and St. Frances. I went to St. Frances myself, so I knew that Rubee would like it, but St. Mary's was dope as well and probably would be more Ray's speed because she was a very inquisitive child. St. Mary's was like a STEM school for little kids, and just from the things that Raylee liked to watch on TV, she would love it. The tuition on St. Mary's was twenty thousand dollars a semester, and I asked Rubee how she would pay for it. This girl told me that she would try to get a voucher as a single mom, and if not, she would ask her cousin, like I wasn't sitting across from her.

She started talking shit about she couldn't ask me to spend forty thousand dollars a year on her child, and it pissed me off, honestly. If I'm your nigga and I can fucking afford it, don't tell me what the fuck I can't spend my money on. Rubee needed to understand that since we were doing what we were doing, Raylee was mine too. Even if Rubee and I stopped fucking around with each other, I'd still pay for school with Raylee because she's a dope kid and deserves all that shit. After she basically told me that she didn't want my help, I shut down on her and stopped talking to her and took Raylee back out to play more games until she got tired.

"You mad at me?" Rubee asked me as soon as we pulled in my driveway.

"Nah, I'm good, Rubee," I replied to her.

I looked in the back seat, and Ray could barely keep her eyes open, making me smile. I got out the car, walked around to open the door for Rubee, and then opened the back seat to get Raylee out.

"She gotta bathe," Rubee reminded me.

"I know."

In the house, I laid Raylee down in the bed while I went to run her a bath. A warm bath was going to put her out like a light. I put some bubbles and some of her toys in the water, even though I was sure she was not going to want to play with them. Rubee had been spending a lot of time over here, so I got Raylee some things to have while she was here. I turned the water off a few minutes later. I walked back into the room, and Rubee was going back and forward with her. She was trying to take her shirt off, but she was whining.

"Lil' girl, you have to take a bath."

"Mama, I don't stank."

"It doesn't matter. You gotta take a bath, Ray. You'll be able to go to sleep as soon as you bathe."

"I don't want to take a bath. I'm sleepy."

"Raylee, big girls have to take baths so you can be squeaky clean. What did you tell me you were earlier when I tried to pick you up to play that game?"

"A big girl," she whispered.

"Right? So, big girls have to get in the tub without their mother telling them to. You want to smell good for your interview tomorrow, right?"

She sleepily nodded her head and launched into my arms. I picked her up and walked her to the bathroom while she laid her head on my shoulder.

"Lil' girl, you got some nerves," Rubee said, following behind us.

After I set Raylee on her feet, I walked out the room and let Rubee and Raylee do their thing. I sat at the desk outside the door and started checking some of my emails when I heard Rubee and Raylee start talking. She must have thought that I left out of the room.

"This water feels good, Mom," Raylee said.

"I know. Kade ran the water just right. Can I ask you something, Ray?"

"Yes."

"How do you feel about Kade? Like, him being with you and me all the time?"

"He makes me laugh. He makes good soup, and he lets me cut things with a knife."

That made me smile.

"Is my daddy coming back? He got you a car for your birthday," Ray asked her mom.

I lowkey held my breath to see what she would say. I still didn't even know how to explain it to her either.

"Someday. Daddy did a bad thing, and he has to go away for a while. When you get older, I'll be able to explain it to you better."

"Okay, Mom. We can be with Kade until my dad comes back."

Who knew that the approval of a four-year-old would make me feel this way?

"Stand up," Rubee instructed her. "What do we say?"

"If anyone touch me here, tell Mommy and Daddy. If anyone touch me here, tell Mommy and Daddy. If anyone touch me here, tell Mommy and Daddy. No one can touch me without my permission," they recited together.

Damn, that really touched me. Rubee may be a hot head who will cut you in a millisecond, but she was a damn good mama. Moments later, Rubee was coming out of the bathroom with Raylee in her arms. She jumped when she saw me.

"Girl! I mean, boy! You scared me!" Rubee squealed.

"I'm neither one of those things," I told her. "Baby girl, you smell good," I told Ray.

"I know. Mommy and me are going to be with you all the time until my daddy gets back. Okay?" she said to me.

I nodded my head and left out of the room while Rubee got her greased up and in her bed clothes. I walked in my room and started the shower. I got undressed, hopped in, and let the hot water run all over me. This shit felt good as hell. Five minutes later, the glass door opened, and Rubee got in with me, and she hugged me from the back.

"Rubee, I don't like how you disrespected me earlier. I want the best for you and Raylee. If the school that's best for Raylee cost a hundred thousand dollars, then I'll pay it. I don't care. Don't underestimate what I would do for the both of you, and don't tell me what I can and can't do. If you got a nigga that can afford it, why should you fix your mouth to ask ya family for money?"

"I mean… I don't want it to seem like I'm using you, bae. Like, we ain't even been together half a damn year. What the hell I look like asking can you pay for her schooling?"

"I get it, but I offered. You ain't asked me shit."

"Okay, I'm sorry," she whispered.

"Whoa? What? Say that again?"

"Shut up. I'm not saying it again. Who do you think I am?"

I turned around and picked her up, prompting her to wrap her arms around my neck and her legs around my waist. I placed my lips on her soft lips, and we started tongue kissing. I loved how she loved to be kissed. She loved when I did a mixture of sucking and biting on her lips. My dick rose up, and I was hard as hell. I need to be inside of her before I lost it.

"Rubee, I need to be inside of you," I whispered in between kissing her.

"Please… please, put it in," she begged.

I moved her back a little and eased inside of her. She closed her eyes as I filled her all the way up.

"Oh my God," she whispered.

She was so damn warm inside. I couldn't fuck her the way I wanted in the shower, so I opened the door, stepped out, and walked into the room while our bodies were still connected. I eased out of her and laid her down on the bed.

"Did you lock the door?" I asked her.

"Yes. She was out like a light before I could finish the first story."

"Good. Open them legs and hold them open," I instructed her.

Eager to get between her legs, I dropped to me knees and started to devour her little pussy. The way I was attacking her clit had her using her thighs as earmuffs for me. I gripped her thighs and pried her legs back open and held on to her thighs. Her pussy lips were swollen because of the way that I was sucking on them. I started tongue fucking her and used one of my hands to start thumbing her clit. She was losing her damn mind, and it was making dick even harder.

"Kadddeeee," she whimpered as she released all over my tongue.

I loved tasting her and loved to smell her when she was turned on. Her scent was intoxicating. After lapping up all of her juices, I kissed up her stomach and stopped on her lips.

"Taste yourself," I whispered to her, before dipping my tongue deep in her mouth, and she happily accepted it.

She started sucking on it like it was a popsicle, while I eased two fingers inside of her warm hole and started to finger fuck her. I dipped the middle finger of my other hand inside of her pussy to get it wet, before I eased it in her ass.

"Oh, Kade," she groaned.

"You like that, beautiful?"

She gripped my arms. "Yes!"

"Oh yeah. Keep your legs open for me, mama."

I started tapping against that G-spot while pushing my finger deeper into her ass, and she put her legs on my shoulders to lift her bottom half off the bed. That was the best position that she could be in because I was about to tap on that other spot. The A-spot. It was a few inches deeper, right in front of the cervix. I started tapping on it, and I watched her eyes close... tight. She arched her back, and her head went back. Her legs were starting to weaken on my shoulders. She was about to give me damn near everything she had to give, and I could tell by the way her stomach started contracted.

"Kade..." she groaned in a lower octave.

"Yeah? What you finna do? Huh? What you finna do, beautiful?"

She grabbed the pillow and slammed it over her face and screamed so loud into it as she squirted all over me.

"Ooowwweee!" She squealed as she continued to squirt.

After her body finished convulsing, I eased my fingers out of her holes and her body fell limp. She was breathing hard as hell. I removed the pillow from her face and tears were streaming down the sides of her face. Her face was red as tomato.

"Mama," I called her and smacked her thigh. "Say something."

"What... the... fuck... was... that, Kade? Kade... please..." she said and started crying even harder.

Her body started shaking again.

"Ma, you straight? Say something, for real. You are scaring me."

"Kade, my body won't stop... Oh my God. You touched something that I ain't never had touched before, and I just can't. Shit! I'm never letting you do that again. That's why I be ready to cut a bitch about you. Now I'mma have to use my gun because if I think you making a bitch squirt from your fingers, all hell is going to break loose, honestly."

I chuckled and laid next to her. "Ma, I'm yours, if you'll have me. You ain't got to worry about other bitches."

"And I'm yours." She sighed.

Turning on my side, I rested my head on my hand and started rubbing my hand up and down her stomach. "You saying we are together?"

She nodded her head. "Ray doesn't mind having you around, and if you are going to be making me nut like that, I'm definitely not going to have a problem having you around."

She pushed me on my back and climbed on top of me. I rested my arms behind my head and stared up at her sexy ass.

"Take that hair down," I instructed her.

She pulled her hair out of the ball it was in and it went everywhere. I loved her sexy ass curls, and I loved running my fingers through that thick shit. She leaned over and started kissing on my neck.

"Mmmm. You know that's my spot, girl," I whispered.

She kissed the other side and then kissed down my abs. She took the head of my dick in her mouth and started sucking on it. I grabbed a pillow and propped up behind it so I could get a good look at my shorty putting in that work. She pulled the head of my dick out of her mouth and then spit on my dick.

"Yeah? You finna get nasty like this, ma?"

She started going ham on my dick. It was like she wouldn't suck another dick again in her life. I reached down and started gripping her hair, and she started going even more crazy. Rubee had my shit wet and sloppy as hell. It was a pool of saliva at the base of my dick, and I had to close my eyes so I wouldn't nut. She started stroking my shit while she was sucking it, and I could feel my hips lifting off the bed.

"Ma... you gotta... ooo..." I groaned as she started sucking on my balls.

She was looking at me while she sucked on my balls and jacked my dick at the same time. Her eyes looked so sexy, and I licked my lips and blew her a kiss. She lifted my balls and started flicking her tongue across that spot, and a wave of pleasure went through my body that made a nigga feel weak as hell.

"Rubee, why you fucking playing with a nigga? You want a nigga crazy over ya lil' young ass, huh?"

She started licking even faster and even started biting it.

"Oh shit!" I hissed. "Damn."

Before I could even let her know that I was nutting, that shit started shooting through the head of my dick like hot lava.

"Ah, damn! Girl. Ah."

She kept going until my dick was flaccid in her hands. She pulled back and kissed my nuts before coming up and kissing my neck again. Now she had me wanting to cry and shit.

"Damn, girl. You gon' make me act up about your lil' ass."

"Uh huh. You got some crazy down in you, boo. It's going to be me that bring it out."

I had a feeling Rubee was going to have me crazy now more than ever. Just the thought of her licking on a nigga the way she just did me made my chest tight.

FRANK

Me and Mayhem were headed toward my other house to talk to Miguel. By now, I was sure Emmanuel was dead. I had the radio blasting because I was sure that he wanted to talk to me about the shit that I told Taiwan, but I didn't. Everything that I told her was the truth. I did think about killing myself often, and I did think that I was a burden to Mayhem and his family… Like now, we were about to go to war with a cartel. He was a family man and didn't need to be in shit like this. He placed his hand on the volume knob and turned it down.

I chuckled. "What's up, man? You don't touch another man's radio."

"What the fuck was Taiwan saying to me? She telling me that you thinking about killing yourself, huh? You think you a burden to me? What the fuck does all of that mean?"

"It's what I said, bruh. It's what I feel."

"I don't understand how you can feel that way because—"

"Because what? Nigga, you grew up in a two-parent home with people who loved you more than anything on this earth. I got a mama and daddy on this earth, and I don't even fucking know where they live. All I get is a stupid mothafuckin' card once a year. You get to experience your parents every day. And please don't get me wrong... I love Mom and Pops with everything in me, and I truly appreciate them for bringing me into y'all family, but it's not the same. It's just not the same. I get one little piece of happiness, bro, one... little... piece, and it's shattered within the blink of an eye. The girl I gave my love to for the last five years fucking shot me and has ran off somewhere. Probably laughing at me because I was a fucking fool. I wanted to marry that girl and give her a kid or two, and this happened. So, yeah, sometimes, I wish I was dead. Yes, I feel like your life would be much better if I was dead," I vented.

"Frank, you are fucking tripping, my nigga, but I can't stop you from feeling the way you feel, but you ain't burdening me at all. You my only friend. My only friend. How the fuck you think I would feel if you took your life? My nigga. I love you. I don't know if I have to tell you that more often so you can feel loved, but you are loved. My kids light up the moment they see you. Malice's kids love they Uncle Frank. My parents call you their third son. How can you say you not loved? Taiwan wants to love your difficult ass. Frank, you got all these people around you who love your light bright ass. And fuck Alex. Fuck Bash. Fuck Kharisma. You a Bailey, nigga. Act like it!"

I ain't have shit to say, but Mayhem kept talking.

"My nigga, do you remember when we first met? You came to school looking like the weight of the world was on your shoulders. You put me in some type of hold that made me want to kill your big head ass. I ain't know saving you from after school detention would result in us being best friends, but it did, and it happened. Right after me and you slept Rickey, what did I tell you? I'll always have your back. Saying that you feel like you a burden to me is hurtful as fuck, honestly. I couldn't even sleep last night, thinking about my best friend wanting to kill himself."

There was a long, drawn out silence between us. I didn't know what to say because I wasn't expecting him to bring up the shit that he said when we killed Rickey. He did tell me that he would always have my back, and that's when I knew that I would die over him because he damn near died over me. I couldn't figure out what to say to him, so I turned the music back up. He ain't say shit else to me until we were pulling up at my crib. We got out and walked around to the door and opened it.

"Close ya eyes, nigga. You know these lights can trigger ya seizures and shit," I joked with Mayhem.

"You gon' get enough of that shit, man," Mayhem said, but he closed his eyes anyway.

My nose hair burned from the horrid stench in the room. I turned the music and lights off and walked over to the cage where Miguel was sleeping.

"Aye! Get up!" I yelled and kicked the bars, making him jump awake.

I opened the cage, pulled him out, and sat him down. I took the earplugs out of his ear, and he looked relieved.

"Mayhem, go get me some water and make some grits for me," I told him.

He walked out of the room and up the stairs into the house. I took the tape off Miguel's mouth and stared at him.

"Where's Romero's hiding spots? You know he sent some killers after me and my lady, and I had to sleep them."

"I don't know. All I know is that he stays in this hotel outside of Chicago. He owns the penthouse."

"Uh huh. In a minute, we are going to call him, and I want a meeting with him. You think that's possible?"

"If you not bringing me, and well..." he said and looked past me at his cousin, who was leaning against the cages, most likely dead, "...him, along with Taiwan, it's not going to go as well as you expect it to."

I nodded my head. Moments later, Mayhem came downstairs with the bowl of grits and bottle of water. I opened the water and gave him a few sips and then gave him a couple of bites of the grits.

"That taste good. How's Taiwan handling everything?"

"She's straight, but make that your last time asking about her. We ain't cool, fam."

The groans in the corner got everybody's attention, and I whipped my head around toward the cage where Emmanuel was being held, and walked over toward him. I used my finger to tap against his forehead, and his eyes opened slowly.

"Oh, you are a trooper. That means you must be of good use to me alive rather than being dead. Hang tight. I'm going to get you some food and water," I said to him, and a tiny look of happiness spread across his face.

"Mayhem, I'll take over from here. Go get this fat nigga some food and shit."

I finished feeding Miguel and then pulled my phone out of my pocket. This phone was untraceable, so he wouldn't be able to tell this location.

"What's his number?" I asked Miguel.

He rattled off the number, and I called the number. He picked up on the first ring.

"Who is this?" he said in his thick ass Italian accent.

"You know who this is," I replied in my best Scarface accent.

"You are playing a dangerous game, young man. All I want is my bitch and my nephews back, and this can all be over," he replied.

"Romero, let's have a meeting. Perhaps we can come to a common ground around this. I'm being generous because I don't normally take meetings with the enemy. It's normally kill first."

"Do you know who I am?" he asked me.

I sighed. "Didn't you ask me that earlier? Look, Romero, are we meeting or not? I got something you want… and you may have some information I need. Let's meet. Chicago Square. Little Tok restaurant, three o'clock sharp, and please… please don't try anything crazy, aight. This my city, so anything might explode," I said right before I hung up the phone.

"You think he gon' try something?" I asked Miguel.

"Honestly, I don't know," he replied.

Mayhem came back downstairs, took the tape off Fat Boy's mouth, and started feeding him. His fat ass was weak, but he wasn't too weak to open his damn mouth to drink that water. That long ass time with no food and water humbled his ass real quick.

"We got a meeting with Romero at three at Lil Tok. Assemble the team. We are taking the fat boy with us," I told Mayhem, and he nodded his head.

Focusing back on Miguel, I said, "So, if I don't kill you, what are your plans? You telling me that you don't fuck with your uncle, but I know how you cartel niggas get down, and I'm extremely paranoid right now. You know the bitch I was gonna marry fucked me over. She was fucking the nigga that worked for me... the whole time. The whole time, Miguel." I started tapping my nose. "Right up under my nose, Miguel. So how I know you wouldn't try to come back and try to get revenge on me killing a bunch of your family members? How I know you wouldn't try to come back and fuck on my woman and shit."

"You can keep me locked up in here for as long as you need to, but give me more food, and more often, I'll be fine, but I was hoping to join my mother in Miami, Florida. My dad banished her away when she tried to leave him," Miguel said.

"Hmm, I see."

Looking at my watch, I saw that it was 1:00 P.M., which meant that we had two hours before we had to be at the meeting. I walked over to the cage and unlocked it, and he fell out onto the floor. I put some fresh tape back on his mouth and put a bag over his head.

"Stand him up," I instructed Mayhem.

I walked over to the corner and hooked the hose up to the faucet and turned it on.

"Watch out, Mayhem."

When he moved, I started spraying his ass down like the pig he was. He wasn't about to be funking up my damn car that I just got fixed from the shootout. Them niggas worked fast on my shit, and it looked brand spanking new. You couldn't even tell that it had been in a shootout just days prior. After I finished hosing him down, I hosed Miguel down too, just for the fuck of it. I was sure he was tired of smelling like piss and shit. They had been down here naked for days.

"We are putting him in the trunk, wet and naked?"

I nodded my head. "There is tarp back there."

Mayhem started leading Emmanuel out of the room, leaving me to deal with Miguel.

"Look, the best I'm going to do for you is keep you in this big cage. Maybe tie your hands behind your back instead of the position they are in now, so you can be just a little bit comfortable. My trust still fucked up, Miguel, so please don't try no silly shit. I won't hesitate to kill you."

"I'm not going to try anything. I know this don't mean shit to you, but you can trust me," he said.

His arms were still in the position of one being thrown over his shoulder, and the other one being behind his back, with his wrists being tied together. I know his arms were going to feel like jelly when I cut him loose. As soon as I cut him loose, he stretched his arms a little bit and then put them behind his back and turned around so I could tie him back up. For some odd reason, I felt like Miguel wasn't lying to me, but my trust was still fucked up, so I was going to be on my P's and Q's with him. After I put him back in the cage, I told him that I was going to come back and feed him tomorrow. I grabbed some things I needed from one of the drawers before locking up the room and going back outside to the trunk of my car.

WAM!

I punched Emmanuel in his nose and knocked him out cold. I turned him on his stomach to get a good look at the wound on his arm. I rubbed some alcohol on it, took my knife off my waist, and made a small incision on the wound. I inserted a tracking device in the wound and rubbed some more alcohol on the wound so it would stop bleeding.

"Was that a tracking device?" Mayhem asked.

I nodded my head. "And this little baby is going to go right under the skin right behind his ear. He's never going to find it or feel it," I said holding up a needle like microphone. "It can withstand a lot of shit."

He chuckled. "You got too much damn money, nigga."

I looked at him and asked, "How you think I always know where you at, Mayhem?"

His smiled immediately turned into a frown. "You put one of those things in my body, Frank? When? Where? How?" He panicked.

"Just chill, nigga. I'm joking."

After I placed the microphone under his skin, I turned him back over on his back and closed the trunk. Today was about to get really interesting.

3:30 P.M.

All our niggas were in place, and we made sure that all of our guys had eyes on all of Romero's niggas. We had been watching him for the last thirty minutes, and he looked as if he was getting impatient. This was going to be good. We came out of our hiding spots and walked into the restaurant. It was crowded, but we had a table smack in the middle of the restaurant. We knew that he had plain clothed men placed strategically in the restaurant, just as we had our plain clothed men placed in there as well. When I approached the table, I held my hand out for him to shake it, but he just stared at it, so I moved my hand up and down as if he shook it and then took a seat.

"Chaz, we meet again," he spoke.

He started the conversation off all wrong, and he wanted to see me sweat, but him calling me Chaz wasn't going to bother me.

"We've never met, so this is not a *we meet again* type thing. Listen, I don't want to hurt you or your family, but how about I give you back the fat one, and you leave Chicago and never come back."

"That wasn't the deal, Mr. Bourne," Romero said, leaning into the table. "Taiwan has been mine ever since she was eighteen. There is no way that she'll ever adjust to being with someone who's not even

AN INSANE LOVE 3

worth ten percent of the money that I bring in. She's expensive and needs things that you just can't give her."

"And what are those things? She may need things that I can't give her, but she definitely *wants* things that *you* can't give her... like a family of her own and marriage. Am I off?"

I could see his jaws flex a little, and he jumped, prompting all of his men to jump up with their weapons, which prompted our men to jump up with their weapons, and his men were outnumbered. The patrons that were of no affiliation to either team jumped up and started screaming. They wanted to leave the restaurant, but both doors were blocked.

"Have a seat, Romero. We are not finished here."

I waved my men down, and Romero slowly sat down, and he waved his men down.

"I can give her those things. Those things just take time."

"Time? Time? You just told me that she's been yours since she was eighteen. She's thirty now. You've had hella time. You just don't like to lose, and that's fine. As a man, I would be sick if I lost that sexy ass woman too."

"New deal. Let me meet with her, and give me one last chance to woo her, and I'll take Emmanuel, and you can keep Miguel."

"Nigga, you smokin' dick. No deal. The only deal is that you get to get Emmanuel and you get to keep your life, Romero. There is no meeting up with Taiwan. You will never see her again, my man."

"No deal then. You said that I may have some information you wanted. What is it?"

"Who told you about me being Chaz?" I asked.

I cared, but at the same time, I didn't. I mean, the person that told him that information so easily could possibly know where my parents are, and they could possibly be in danger. My parents are old as shit now, and I am 1,000 percent sure that they can't move the way they used to move.

"Wouldn't you like to know." He smirked. "Let me meet with Taiwan."

I laughed. "I don't give a fuck that much, bro. It's all good. I'm going to give you Emmanuel, but only if you agree to leave us the fuck alone and we move on."

Whether he agreed to leave us alone or not, I was still going to give him Emmanuel because I needed the information that the tracker and listening device was going to provide me. I picked up my phone and called the guy who had Emmanuel.

"Bring him in," I said into the phone and hung up.

Moments later, my guy was walking Emmanuel's naked ass through the restaurant, with the bag over his head, and his arms still bound behind his back. Romero's eyes grew large when he noticed his nephew didn't look nothing like he last saw him. Starving him over the last few days had that nigga looking bad as fuck.

He jumped up, and then Mayhem jumped up. "What did you do to him? Where is Miguel?"

"Not so fast, you cocker spaniel looking ass nigga. Agree to leave us the fuck alone, and you get Emmanuel. If not, he's going to walk back out the door, and you'll never see him again."

"How do I know Miguel's not dead?"

"He's not. All you have is my word."

"Okay... Okay... I'll leave you alone. Just let my..." He swallowed. "Just let my nephew go."

"Romero... all you have is your word. You say that you are going to leave us alone, and I'm trusting that you will. If not, everybody is going to die. Remember that, okay?"

"Fuck you!" he hissed.

I stood up and held my hand out to shake on the deal. "Usually, deals end with a handshake."

"Fuck you!"

"Let him go," I told the guy who was holding Emmanuel, and his men got him and then held onto him.

Romero stood and pulled out a cigar and lit it. He pulled on it a few times before blowing smoke my way. "You can have Miguel. I know he turned on me. He's been hating me since I jacked him up for trying to fuck on Taiwan. He thought I was stupid. I knew he was checking her out when I wasn't looking."

"So what you saying to me right now is that you are about to renege on the deal?"

"It'll be over my dead body before you marry Taiwan and get her pregnant. I'll kill her before that happens," he growled.

I leaned into him and whispered, "Then over your dead body, it will be. Good day, Romero."

Me and Mayhem walked out of the restaurant, with our men right behind us. We had several plans in place. Romero was fucking with the right fucking crew.

ROMERO

The moment that Frank, Mayhem, and his crew cleared the restaurant, I ordered some of my men to tail them. I hated that I had to admit to myself that I wasn't prepared to deal with the Baileys. Frank was not a regular mulligan. This young man was damn near bionic and was prepared for it all. As much digging as I did, I couldn't find a single address of anyone he was close to on file. Even that bitch that told me Frank was the product of two spies couldn't tell me anything more than that. I hadn't even heard from her since. I was pretty sure she was dead, because she gave out too much information over the airways, and they were always listening.

"Get Emmanuel some clothes to cover up," I ordered my men.

One of them came out of their jackets for him to put on. Emmanuel didn't even look the same. He looked like he lost thirty pounds in the body and the face. He fell in the seat next to me and fell against my shoulder.

"What did he do to you?" I asked him.

"I need food. I need food." He groaned.

"Okay, we are going to get you cleaned up at the hotel," I told him.

Two hours later

Emmanuel had been checked out, cleaned up, and was now sitting across from me eating and drinking like he hadn't been fed in years. I kept staring at him because I was waiting on him to tell me something about this dude that was going to help me get my bitch back. Truth is, I was missing Taiwan like shit. I missed kissing her lips. I missed being inside of her, and the thought of that ugly mulligan being inside of her had me weak to my stomach. When I got her back, I was going to have to scrub her with bleach just to get his scent off her. She could have been with any dude she wanted to be with, but she had to get with him. *Him* of all people. I knew that he was going to be a problem the day that I saw him kiss her on her neck, and I saw her knees get weak. Her knees never got weak when she was with me. Damn! I had the perfect chance to kill him, but she told me that I didn't have anything to worry about as if I didn't find her journal describing in detail how she loved the feel of the piercings on his dick when she was sucking it. Detailing how he couldn't even fit inside of her. That made me feel inadequate as fuck because I knew for a fact that he was packing just like they said black dudes be.

My phone started ringing, and I looked down to see that it was Essie. I knew the reason that she was calling, and I wasn't prepared to deal with her right now, but I had to. I stepped out on the balcony to answer the phone.

"Essie," I answered the phone.

"Are you fucking serious? Are you fucking serious? Romero Santiago!" she screamed into the phone.

"Essie—"

"No! You are really trying to divorce me to get married to that girl."

"It's not like—"

"I'm telling your father. He would kill you before he let you marry that girl, and you know that. You are out of your goddamn mind if you think that you will just up and leave me for that girl... her of all girls."

"Can I speak?" I said.

"Hell fucking no, you can't speak! What do you have to say? Huh? What the fuck do you have to say?"

"Essie. I love her. If I have to stay in Chicago to be with her, then that's what I'll do."

"I can't believe you are saying this to me. Your wife. The mother of your sons. My father is not going to be happy when he hears this."

"Whatever, Essie. Sign the papers and get your ten million a year. You can be with your boy toy, and I get to be with Tai."

"You're delusional!" she screamed and hung up the phone.

I sighed and went to the website where I met Taiwan. I kept looking at the website every day, trying to see if I could find another girl, but none of them could hold a candle to Taiwan. I typed her name in, and her profile was still up, and I smiled at the eighteen-year-old profile pic of Taiwan smiling back at me. At eighteen, her body was perfect. Her smile was perfect. Everything about her was perfect, and we would have been just fine had her hoe of a friend not gone missing. I smiled at the thought I had in my head. She was going to be contacting me soon.

I stepped back inside, and Emmanuel's ass was still eating.

I sat back in my seat. "You ready to talk?"

"That moolie is a sadist or something. He kept us locked in cages that you could barely turn around in. He kept the damn room ice cold. Ice fucking cold, and we were naked against steel bars, Uncle Romero. He flashed some fluorescent ass lights, and he played very loud heavy metal music in intervals of twenty. The music was loud."

"Spy tactics," I whispered to myself. "And you snitched, didn't you? Rolled right over, didn't you?"

"No, but my bitch made ass cousin rolled over, and he still got treated like shit. I'm killing him if I ever see him again. He's not fit to do anything in the Santiago Cartel."

I nodded my head. I always knew Miguel wasn't cut out for this shit. That's why I gave him something simple to do in the organization like drive my baby around. I'm not surprised he rolled over though. I'm 1,000 percent sure that he's just trying to get to his mama in Florida.

"How are we going to get back at him?" Emmanuel asked.

"I don't know."

"What you mean, you don't know? He's disrespected us one too many times today."

I was getting ready to respond to him when my phone went off. I opened it, and it was a video attachment from an unknown number. I opened the video, and a lump appeared in my throat the size of Texas. The men I had tailing Frank and Mayhem were naked and kneeling, with their hands tied behind their back with tape over their mouths. In the background, I could see a cage that Emmanuel was telling me about. Frank was a diabolical, and I was going to enjoy killing him. I was going to enjoy every fucking moment of it.

"You gave me your word, Romero." Frank appeared into the camera. He pointed a long ass sword toward the camera. "You gave me your fucking word, and this is what you do? Now I'm about to show you what I'm truly about," he said, and then called my nephew's name. "Miguel."

"Son of a bitch!" I growled and slammed my hand on the table.

Miguel appeared next to the men with a long sword in his hand. The fucking sword looked like something right out of a fucking movie. I could tell that shit was sharp just from the damn video.

"Miguel, look at the camera and then show your uncle what happens when he fucks with one of us?" Frank said.

Us. Miguel is a fucking traitor.

Emmanuel got up and walked around the table to look at the video with me.

"When you... when you fuck with one of us, this is what happens,"

Miguel stuttered out, before swinging the sword in a downwards motion and chopped the man's head off, and blood started spurting out of the headless body before he fell over. I closed my eyes slowly before opening them again.

"Hmmm." Frank groaned. "Did you hear that, Romero? Shit sounded so damn good. Miguel. Next man. Go faster this time."

I watched as Miguel chopped off the next five dudes' heads with no mercy, and my stomach turned, but I couldn't turn the video off. I felt as if I was going to have a heart attack because I couldn't believe my men had been so careless like this and gotten caught. Damn, I had to fucking remember that this fucking moolie was raised this way. He knew I wasn't going to leave him alone, so he was prepared.

"I told you that nigga was a fucking sick ass sadist. I told you, Unc. I won't rest until he is dead. I'm going to torture him. I'm going to slash him with that same damn—"

"Shhhh," I shushed him.

"Romero, this last guy…" Frank said and paused. He picked up whatever he was recording on and walked toward the back of the room. The camera panned down as he walked through the blood on the floor. "Look at all that blood. Umph, umph, umph." The blood kicked up on his boots, and it made me sick. Once he made it to the back of the room, I heard a small click, and a light came on. My heart felt like it could explode as tears sprang into my eyes.

"Say hi to daddy, Romero Jr.," Frank said.

My son was torn up and barely recognizable. Both of his eyes were swollen closed, his nose was busted, and both of his lips were split wide open. He was locked in that small ass cage like a rat. Frank then got next to him, and the camera was on both of them. My nostrils flared.

"Look, I know what you're thinking, Romero…" He paused before chuckling, *"I'm going to kill that moolie,"* he said in a fake ass Italian accent. "Your son here taught me that before I whooped his ass. Moolie is an Italian word for nigga, and I think that's cool. Now, there is a new deal on the table. You can get your son back, because he is of no use to me, but you have to promise to leave me and my family alone. I've shown you what I'm capable of. I... just... wanna... be... left... alone. I'll call you soon."

The video cut off.

"What are we going to do? We have to call Grandpa, Unc. He'll know what to do," Emmanuel said.

My dad wasn't going to help me do anything because as far as he was concerned, I got myself into this mess, and I was going to have to get myself out. I could have just taken the easy way out, but I was not going to let this punk scare me. If he wanted a war, he was going to get one.

ALICIA TAYLOR

"Honey, come to bed," Gavin said from the door.

"I can't. I can't get his fucking face out of my brain, Gav," I replied as I looked at all of the newspapers clippings on the board.

Gavin walked further into the room and placed his hand on my shoulders and slowly massaged them. "You've been unofficially working this case since you were fourteen, Alicia. You can't let this consume you anymore. You have to work on the Santiago case and get it over with, because you are supposed to retire right after."

"Gav, he looks just like my brother-in-law. I know it's him! I know it's him! Frank is Malcolm Jr.!" I stressed.

"All you have to go on is that baby picture, Alicia. What are you going to do? Ask him to see his stomach to see if he got a birthmark on it?"

"I'm going to take this baby picture somewhere and have someone age it thirty or so years, like they be doing those missing children. If Frank is who I think he is, he should be thirty-six."

"Alicia…"

"No, Gavin."

"This is what happened the last time you thought you had a lead.

You drove yourself sick, and I don't want to see you like that anymore. Now, come to bed! I'm not going to ask you again!" my husband growled before walking out of the room.

Gavin Taylor and I grew up together in a time where interracial relationships were frowned upon. They still are, but at least we have more rights than we did. We've been friends since middle school, and it grew into love when he was all I had to lean on when my sister, her husband, and my nephew were killed in what the police said was a murder-suicide. My parents believed every word of it because they hated that Annette had snuck off and married Malcolm Bennett. Malcolm loved my sister and her son, Joshua. He loved her so much that Malcolm had adopted Joshua and raised him as his own. The 'murder-suicide' of my sister and her family is the reason that I became a police officer and worked my way up the ranks until I got in with the FBI.

The case was always fishy to me because, like I said before, Malcolm loved my sister and her son, and they were so excited to be expecting a baby because they had been trying forever. So when she finally got pregnant, everyone was happy but my parents. Malcolm's parents died in a car accident right after he graduated from high school, so my sister was all he had. Malcolm had made so many videos of him talking to my sister's stomach, and plenty more of them when Malcolm Jr., or MJ as they called him, was born. I stopped watching them decades ago, but not before I had them transferred to DVDs since camcorders were becoming obsolete.

I was a freshman in high school when this tragedy struck. The tapes were the only things I had left of my sister and her family. I said this case struck me as weird because in the report, it said that Malcolm was drunk when he killed his wife and son, but that wasn't true because Malcolm didn't even drink. My sister didn't drink either, not even a glass of wine, but according to the reports, there were glasses of alcohol all over the place. The report also said that Malcolm shot Josh first, then Annette, and then himself, which was false, because Malcolm was a journalist and didn't even own a gun. I didn't care what the reports said.

The case got even stranger because they only mentioned Malcolm Jr. once. Once. They only mentioned my baby nephew once, and then they acted like he never existed... acted like the whole family never existed. It was like they never even searched for him. For years, I went up to the police station, asking if there was any lead about my nephew missing, and they brushed me off and told me the case was no longer in their hands, and the government had picked it up, which made the case even stranger. Why would the government pick up a murder suicide case of a journalist and his wife? All of that led me to believe that Malcolm had picked up on something that he wasn't supposed to, and they got rid of him. That had always been my theory, but that didn't make sense to me because why would they take Malcolm Jr., and his body never show up, ever? No bones or nothing. I kept researching and researching, until one day, all of Malcolm Sr.'s articles disappeared from the web. I couldn't find anything that he had ever worked on, and that bothered me.

After so long of hitting roadblock after roadblock, I had given up, but after seeing Frank's face in the restaurant that day, I knew... knew that he was Malcolm Jr. I was going to feel like shit if he'd been here all his life and I just didn't search hard enough for him. If he had been here all his life, then how come he never came up in none of the foster care systems? I searched thousands of pictures and never found any picture that looked remotely close to him. I knew that he was going to curse me out, but the next time that I saw him, I was going to let him know my findings. I just hoped that Romero didn't get to him before I could.

I shut the light off in the room and walked into my bedroom to join my husband in bed.

"I thought I was going to have to come get you, young lady," Gavin said, making me smile.

After a few moments of silence, I said, "I'm afraid that Romero might get to Malcolm Jr. before I can." I sighed.

"Alicia, you don't even know if that's Malcolm Jr. or not. Do not blow your last case on this. You're going to retire at fifty with a perfect record. You need to stay focused."

I'd been with the FBI since I was thirty years old, and I had put in the work for twenty years, and it was now time for me to retire. My record was perfect, but this last case with The Santiago Cartel had been giving me the blues for the last few years. The case was handed over to me after the first agent got outed and killed by them. I had been doing my due diligence, but they were smart. When I had the chance to get Taiwan by herself, I thought that I was going to have me a mole, but that changed, and I felt like I was back at square one.

Me and Gavin's kids were grown and had families of their own, and after I retired, I was going to spend more time with them. My job always had me on the go, but Gavin held down the kids and the house, and that was why I loved this man more than anything on this earth.

"Goodnight, Gavin," I whispered, knowing that he was already sleep.

Like I had been doing every night for the last few nights, I stared at the ceiling and tried to count sheep. It was going to be hard since my nephew was on mind really bad. I knew that was my nephew, and no one was going to be able to tell me any different, not even Gavin.

TAIWAN

A FEW DAYS LATER

It had been a few days since Frank told me that he met with Romero and it didn't go so well. He didn't give me any of the specifics; he just told me that the meeting didn't go well, and he was going to have to knock that nigga off his feet. I was thankful that he was keeping me out of it because after that shootout in the middle of the fucking highway, I didn't care to know anything else about his gangsta lifestyle.

It was noon, and I was standing in the bathroom mirror getting ready to do something that I hadn't done in years, and that was go and see my parents. I couldn't remember the last time I had seen them. I just wanted to talk to them and let them know that I was back for good. I wanted to have a relationship with them again. I hoped that we could forgive each other and start over because at this point, I was much like Frank—the Bailey family was all I had, especially with Tristan being in jail.

Ding.
Ding.
Ding.
Ding.

I sighed because I had been getting these weird emails for the last

AN INSANE LOVE 3

couple of days. They all were asking me what my prices were for nasty ass shit that I hadn't done in years. I opened up the first one and I screamed.

From: Luv2Fuck@gmail.com
Tai, how much to suck on this pretty little asshole?

I screamed again, and Frank ran into the bathroom with his gun in his hand, ready to shoot it. Embarrassed, I closed my phone and set it down on the sink and swiped at the tears that were rolling down my face.

"Baby, what's wrong?" Frank asked. "Why you crying?"

"Frank..." I cried.

He pulled me into his chest and rubbed his hand up and down my back.

"Tai, tell me what's going on?"

"I fucked up. Things I've done when I was eighteen years old are coming back to haunt me," I told him as I cried.

"What you mean..." Frank paused and pulled his phone out of his pocket and pecked on it a few times before saying, "Oh shit!"

"What?"

"Shut your Instagram account down, now!" he ordered me.

I opened up my account, and the same picture that I just got in my email was on my IG account, alone with some other racy pictures that I had taken for Romero. I quickly deactivated my account, even though the pictures already had fifty thousand likes on it. Fifty thousand people had seen my asshole.

"My life is over, Frank! My goodies were on display for all my followers to see," I whispered and tried to slide down to the floor, but he caught me.

"Look, you sexy as fuck, and you ain't going to lose no followers behind that shit. When you get your page up and running again, it's going to be hella niggas following you. You just have to let them know that you got a crazy ass nigga that'll find out where they live and break they neck in real life," Frank said, trying to make the situation better.

He took another phone out of his pocket and placed it on the counter. He pressed a couple of buttons before placing it on speaker. Moments later, the voice that came over the line made me hold my breath.

"Ahh, how did you like that pretty asshole?" Romero said into the speaker.

"Actually, I love it. I was just sucking on it last night. Damn near sucked a fart out of that butt," Frank replied, making me hit him in his chest, but he wasn't lying.

Romero let out a low growl. "Give me my son, and you can keep Miguel's bitch ass."

"Nah, since you wanna act like a bitch and post my girl's naked photos for the world to see, I think I'll keep him a little longer."

Romero was talking, but the only thing I was focusing on was the fact that Frank had started unbuckling his pants and freeing his monster. It was crazy that the sight of it always made my mouth water and my pussy wet. He turned me around, bent me over the sink, and eased inside of my pussy, making me moan really loud.

"You hear that, bitch ass nigga? That's me... making my girl moan. Fucking her in that very hole you posted for the world to see," he said, lying like shit.

Frank wasn't getting anywhere near my ass with that big ass dick. I had to be drunk off my ass to let him fuck me in my ass.

"Taiwan, baby, can you hear me?" Romero called out to me, but Frank was now beating my walls down, and I couldn't believe I was as turned on as I was.

"Answer him, Tai," Frank instructed me.

"Ye-yes, I can hear you."

"All you have to do is come home, baby, and I won't do what I'm about to do next. Please. I've started the divorce proceedings with Essie. Do you know even know who you are with right now? You are with a man who gets off on killing people. Taiwan, he keeps people in cages, and you are going to be next. He don't care about—"

"Shit! Girl! Who's my nasty ass bitch?" Frank groaned. "You wet as fuck! Throw it back."

AN INSANE LOVE 3

"I'm your nasty bitch, Frank!" I moaned as I was getting close to nutting.

"Taiwan, I can give you what he can't, and you know it!" Romero hissed, clearly getting frustrated. "His name ain't even Frank, did you know that?"

"You can't give her this nut about I'm about to give her," Frank groaned. "Tell Chaz that you are about to cum, baby. Tell him."

"Oooowwwee, Chaz, I'm cummmmiinnnnggg," I moaned as I came all over his dick.

He eased out of me, and I could feel his cum dripping out of me.

"That was the one, bae. That was Lil' Frank, right there."

"Taiwan!" Romero yelled my name. "You're going to be sorry that you ever crossed me."

"Yeah, yeah, yeah," Frank said and hung up the phone.

After me and Frank got cleaned up, we left the guesthouse and walked up the sidewalk to Mayhem's house. As usual, the kitchen door was open. We walked in, and Mayhem had Olena on the counter, kissing all over her. A few minutes later, we would have caught an eye full.

Olena hopped off the counter and straightened herself up. "I was just about to come and see you because of your fucking Instagram. What the hell happened? Who hacked you? Wait, where are y'all about to go?"

"Girl, Romero is trying to make my life a living hell, and I'm going to my parents' house. I think it's time that we had a conversation. It's been years, and I was hoping that I can get them to tell Tristan to put me back on the visitation list. It's been too long."

"Taiwan, are you sure you want to do this? You know the last time you seen them, your dad was getting his ass whooped by them Italians. You want me to come with you for support?"

"The fuck you think I'm standing right here for?" Frank growled.

"Watch yo' mouth, nigga!" Mayhem growled back.

"You trying to take it outside?" Frank asked and pointed at the door with his thumb.

"Shut up, nigga. What y'all doing when you get back? My wife wanna get out the house with the kids and shit?"

"It's whatever. We gon' have to shut that bitch down because I don't have time to be trying to keep my eyes on every mothafucka in that bitch."

"Aight, bet. Let me make a few calls, and everything should be set in place."

"Bet that up," Frank replied.

We walked out to the front to Frank's car, and he opened the door for me. He walked around to the other side and got in and started the car. Once we were cruising down the road, I looked him up and down, and I don't think I'll ever be able to get over how fine he was. He had on a white pair of Levi jeans with a plain white tee and a pair of white and gold Air Jordans. He had on a white and gold snapback to the back. He hadn't had a hair cut in a while, so his defined curls were sticking up a little. I rolled my eyes a little at the fact that he still hadn't got that bitch's name covered up.

"What's up? Why you be staring at me like that?"

"You ugly."

"Ahhh, that's real."

"Nah, you fine as fuck. I love looking at you just like you like looking at me."

He nodded his head.

"Frank, can I ask you a question?"

"Depends."

"On what?"

"Just ask."

"Are you white?"

"I'm not that fucking light skinned, mothafucka. Do you see this hair? This shit kinky as hell. My parents are black, bae." He laughed.

"How did Romero find out you were Chaz?"

"Good question. He didn't tell me, but I don't give a fuck. The only thing that crossed my mind was if my parents were in danger. If they were, they can take care of themselves. They grown."

I felt like he was getting a little pissed, so I stopped talking about it.

He grabbed my hand and kissed it and then placed it on his lap. It gave me butterflies when he did certain things like this. It made me feel loved.

After a few moments of silence, he said, "Yeah, I could see myself falling in love with you, Tai. That was the last question you asked me the other day," Frank said. "A nigga ain't going to lie, I'm scared like shit because of that shit that happened with Alex, but I know I can't make you pay for something that you haven't done yet. I'm telling you now, you ever pull a gun on me, you better hit me with a kill shot, or—"

"You gonna put me in the box again?"

"You ain't going to let that go, are you?"

"No! You don't know how that..." He cut his eyes at me, making me clamp my lips together. "Never mind," I whispered.

"It's all good, ma."

This question had been burning in the back of my mind. I was scared to ask because I knew how blunt Frank could be when it came to shit, and I didn't want my feelings hurt.

"Just ask, Tai. You look like you got a question ready to fly past those big ass dick suckers on your face."

"Do you care about my past?" I asked quickly.

"Nah. You did what the fuck you had to do, and plus, you weren't fucking niggas that worked for me, so we good. I know for a fact I'm not going to run into a nigga that you fucked. Wait... or am I?"

"I hadn't fucked many niggas, Frank. Matter of fact, you are the second black guy that I have fucked. I was fucking my first for a lil' while, and then that's when I became a... you know, and then it was Romero, and maybe a couple—"

"Ma! It's all good." He laughed.

We rode in silence for the rest of the way until we pulled onto the street that I grew up on. Nothing much had changed about the road. A couple more houses had been built, but other than that, it still looked good. Frank pulled up to the curb and parked the car. He waited for a second and then got out to open the door for me. My heart was beating so fast because I wondered how different my parents looked now. They were both in their early sixties.

"You ready, ma?" Frank asked, and I nodded my head. "You look good, baby. Don't think too much about this shit because they can either welcome you with open arms or not. Aight?"

I nodded my head. We walked up on the porch hand in hand. Just when I was getting ready to knock on the door, the door came open slightly, like we were on a scary movie or some shit. Frank raised his shirt and pulled his gun from his waist.

"Wait right here, ma. Do not come in here until I tell you to," Frank ordered me.

Frank eased the door open with his foot and walked inside. I knew something bad had happened. I could feel it in the pit of my stomach.

"FUCK! I'mma kill that bitch!" Frank hollered.

I rushed into the house, and he was standing at the entryway of the kitchen.

"Bae, don't—" he started, but it was too late. I was at his side.

I started screaming. I was screaming at the top of my lungs. My parents' bodies were sitting at the table, but their heads were sitting on the fucking kitchen table. I walked close to the table, slipping all over the blood. The men that were supposed to be watching them were laying headless on the other side of the kitchen.

"Bae, come on. Let's get out of here."

"We can't leave them!" I screamed.

Beep. Beep. Beep.

Frank walked further into the kitchen and started looking around.

"SHIT!" he shouted.

He didn't say another word as he scooped me up like I was a rag doll and rushed out of the house. Frank leaped off the porch like he was Superman and landed on his back, me on top of him, and then rolled over and placed his body on top of mine, placing his heavy hands over my ears.

BOOM!

My parents' house had blown up, and Frank had protected me by covering my body with his huge body, and my eardrums by covering them with his big hands.

One hour later

There were fire trucks, police cars, and ambulances everywhere. The blue and red lights were damn near blinding me. Me and Frank were sitting in the back of an ambulance after getting checked out after the police finished questioning us. We both had minor scratches on us, and Frank's back was in pain, but other than that, we were okay, physically. Mentally, I was fucked up. My fucking parents had their fucking heads chopped off. I'd never get that picture out of my head.

"Aye! Shit! Y'all straight!" Mayhem had jumped in the back of the ambulance. "They finally let me on the damn street. I left Olena at home with the kids. What the *fuck* happened?"

Mayhem sat next to me, and I leaned on his shoulder. He wrapped his arm around me. "I'mma kill that cocker spaniel ass nigga," Frank said.

I looked up at him with tears in my eyes. "Frank, are you sure that Romero did this? He wouldn't kill my parents, Frank. He just wouldn't do that." I cried.

Frank looked at me with fire in his eyes. "What the fuck are you saying to me, Taiwan? Who the fuck else could have done it? Ohh, I get it! Why you think Romero wouldn't kill your parents? Because he loves you too much? That's the perfect reason for him to do the shit because love will make you do some crazy things. Trust me... I fucking know!" Frank snapped and stood up. "I need some air."

I grabbed his hand. "Frank. Please don't leave me. Please."

He snatched away from me, but he sat back down. He pulled a phone out of his pocket and handed it to me. "Call him. Call him and see what the fuck he says! Put it on speaker."

With shaky hands, I slowly but surely dialed Romero's number and put it on speaker. After a few rings, he picked up.

"Thought I'd be hearing from you."

"Romero..." I called his name. "Please..." My voice squeaked. "Please tell me you didn't murder my parents."

Romero paused, and I looked up at Frank. "Baby girl... I love you. I love you more than anything on this earth, but... the game is the game. Come the fuck home or your brother is next. You think that boy cares about you... he doesn't. If he did, he would let you come back to me. If he cared about you, he wouldn't have started a war. I won't stop until you're back in my arms, Taiwan... either by choice or by force. If it's the latter, you won't like me very much. See you soon," Romero spat and hung up the phone.

I let out a gut-wrenching scream, making Mayhem hold me tighter. My parents were gone, and I was going to lose my brother too if I didn't go back to Italy with Romero. I cried at at the fact that I was about to lose everyone that I had left. Through misty eyes, I could see that Frank was glaring at me with his nostrils flaring, and his jaws were clenching. His pupils were doing that thing they did while we were at the restaurant before we left and got into the shootout. His head was moving slowly from side to side, and his eyes were turning red.

"Frank..." Mayhem called his name, and snapped his fingers, but he ignored him. "Frank... come back to us. Can you hear me? Frank," Mayhem queried, but he didn't budge.

"Frank..." I called his name.

We got nothing. He was still in the same position, and it was starting to scare me. He was in the deepest zone that I had seen anyone in before. I moved away from Mayhem's shoulder and reached across the ambulance and touched his knee.

"Taiwan, don't—"

It was too late. Frank caught my wrist, twisted it around and almost broke my arm. He had my wrist so tight that I was yelping out in pain, and it still didn't break him out of the trance he was in. Mayhem reacted quickly by wrapping his hands around Frank's neck, cutting his air supply off. Moments later, Frank inhaled sharply, and Mayhem let him go. Frank looked down at me and then let me go. I fell to the floor and scooted away from him.

He tried to approach me. "Did I hurt—"

"Take a walk, Frank," Mayhem instructed him.

He looked at me with pleading eyes before he hopped out of the ambulance and started walking down the street.

"Mayhem... what happened?"

"First, never touch him when he's under like that because he could have killed you."

"Under?"

"Trust me. It was nothing toward you. He didn't know it was you until I brought him back. When he gets really pissed off, he goes into a deep trance. Sometimes he can come right out of it, and sometimes he can't, but under no circumstances do you touch him when he's like that. It's some shit his parents did to him, and that's one thing that he's never told me, so I don't know."

"That's why," I whispered as Mayhem helped me up and put me back on the seat.

"What are you talking about?"

"That's why he feels like he a burden to you, Mayhem."

"He ain't no burden to me. He rarely gets mad like that. When all of this shit is over with, he'll be fine. I promise. Let's go find him."

Mayhem hopped out of the ambulance and then helped me down. We started walking down the street, and I heard my name being called.

"Taiwan!"

I turned around to see Alicia running up on me.

"Not now!" I said to her when she finally caught up with us.

"We really need to talk," she urged.

"I don't feel like talking about that bastard right now. I need to find my man before he does something crazy."

She stopped walking and let me and Mayhem continue our trek.

"Frank!" Mayhem called out to him.

I swear it felt like we had walked a mile before we found in him an alleyway, sitting against the wall with his knees pulled into his chest, and he was staring straight ahead. Mayhem held his hand up to stop me at the corner of the alley.

"Frank... you okay?" Mayhem asked him.

He shook his head 'no'. "I could have killed her. I could have killed her. I'm tired of this," he replied lowly, but I could hear him.

"She understands, Frank. Come on, let's go home."

"I need to be alone. I can't be around her right now."

"Where are you going to go?"

He shrugged his shoulders. "I just need to be alone for a lil' while."

Mayhem waved me over, and I slowly walked over to him. I squatted in front of him, and he opened his legs a little so I could get closer to him. Afraid to look at me, he held his head down. I grabbed his chin and made him look at me.

"I hurt you," he whispered.

"I understand, Frank."

"No, you don't! I think we need to separate for a little while. Just until—"

"Until what, Frank? Until what?"

He shrugged his shoulders.

"What am I supposed to do while you're gone? You're going to let me go through this alone?"

"I'm doing more bad than good right now. I just need time. You stay at Mayhem's, and don't go anywhere without security. I'll be around."

"What about your security, Frank? Who's going to be around to protect you? What if something happens to you? I can't... please," I pleaded.

Frank stood up and then helped me to my feet. He grabbed my cheeks and placed a small kiss on my lips and pulled back.

"I'll be good, ma. I'll be good."

"Frank..."

He shushed me by placing his lips back on mine and then pushing his tongue in my mouth. I happily accepted it. Moments later, he pulled away and wiped the tears away that were falling down my eyes. He placed a kiss on my forehead before he walked around me and dapped Mayhem up. He handed me his car keys and then started down the alleyway.

"Mayhem, where is he going?" I whispered as I continued to watch him.

"Underground. He about to fuck some shit up."

Two weeks later
The funeral

I couldn't believe that I was sitting in front of my mom's and dad's caskets. I felt numb. Olena and Mayhem had been doing everything to try and cheer me up, but nothing worked. I wish that I could have gotten a call or even a text from him, letting me know that he was okay, but I didn't get anything. I kept calling back to back, but I wasn't getting through. I kept bugging Mayhem to see if he had called or text him, but he told me that he hadn't. Mayhem told me that it could be weeks before he would hear from him. He said when Frank goes underground, he turns into a different animal, but he'd be fine.

It took so long for the medical people to release my parents' bodies that I wanted to get them cremated, but they already had their plans made out with the funeral home, and I didn't want to disrespect that. The church was packed out. Mayhem had security so heavy that you would have thought that it was a concert going on inside of the church. I was scared to look around the church because when we walked in, I was getting all types of dirty stares. This case wasn't national news like when Kam's dad went to jail, but they did have all my business out there. They had made Facebook groups about what really happened to my parents and how I was the cause of their death. I guess they weren't lying. It also didn't help that my parents always did shit around Chicago. One theory was that my money had dried up from the sugar daddy, so I killed my parents for insurance money. I had to deactivate my page because the messages started getting out of control.

As soon as the preacher started doing the eulogy, the doors of the church opened, and I slightly turned my head to see who it was, and it was Alicia escorting Tristan in. I didn't even know that he was coming. I jumped up and ran toward him. I wrapped my arms around him and started crying so hard.

"Go back to your seat, Taiwan. Tristan has to stay back here," she said, and I finally looked him up and down.

They still had the chains on his ankles and on his wrists, but they were in front of him. I looked at her like she had shit on her face. She still had my brother in these cuffs like he was a danger to anyone in here.

"My brother is not an animal. You can take those chains off him," I snapped.

"Hey. Calm down. It's protocol. Go back to your seat. I'll see you afterwards," he whispered and nodded his head.

I turned around to see Korupt holding his hands out to me. I placed my small hand into his, and he walked me back to my seat. The rest of the funeral, I could barely sit still. After the funeral, the funeral directors led the caskets out, and the family filed out of the rows and got behind the directors. To avoid the stares, I kept my head down. Alicia already had Tristan outside, and I got a good look at him in the sun. He had changed drastically. He was much bigger and had a full thick beard now. He had on a white button down and a pair of slacks paired with some black dress shoes. The prison must have provided those clothes. He looked me up and down and then I hugged him again.

Tristan and I had a typical big brother and sister relationship. We

AN INSANE LOVE 3

loved each other more than anything in this world, but we also fought a lot, yet I wouldn't change it for the world. He looked me up and down before raising his arms up, and I went under them and hugged him. His arms were resting on my shoulders. He placed a kiss on my forehead, and I fell to pieces again.

"We are going to be good, baby sis," he reassured me.

"I always knew that girl's lifestyle was going to catch up with her," someone said.

I turned around to see one of my mom's colleagues walking by us.

"Alright now, don't let these cuffs fool you, family. Keep yo' thoughts inside ya mothafuckin' head," Tristan growled, and the man scurried along.

"Mr. Dalton. Calm down," Alicia said.

I looked at her. "Can he ride with us to the burial? Please?" I begged.

"No, but you can ride with us."

I turned around to look at Mayhem, and he was shaking his head 'no'. I sighed and looked from Alicia back to Mayhem, while he was still shaking his head 'no'.

"There is enough room in our car for both Alicia and Tristan," Olena said, and I looked at Alicia, hoping that she would say yes.

"I'm breaking protocol, but Dalton is a good inmate, so I trust that he won't do anything crazy," Alicia said.

On the way to the funeral burial, it was quiet. Olena had put the kids in the truck with Korupt and Angela.

"Can somebody tell me what's going on? I was moved to solitary a week or so ago and nobody is telling me what's going on. Does this have something to do with my parents' murders or what?" Tristan asked.

I cleared my throat. "Romero killed them, and he threatened you next, so Mayhem had you moved. We just want you safe."

"Wait, the nigga you were fucking with? Why would he do that?" he asked me and then looked at Mayhem. "Are you handling this?"

Mayhem looked from him to Alicia, and Tristan got the hint. After that small exchange, the rest of the way to the burial was quiet with the exception of Tris and I making small talk.

Many people didn't come to the burial, and I was happy. After the pastor committed both of their bodies to the ground, I got up to put roses on both of their caskets as they were lowered into the ground. When I took my seat, my phone went off. I pulled it out, and it was a text message from an unknown number.

Unknown: *Baby, you look beautiful. Don't know if that's something you say to someone the day of their parents' funerals. I wish that I could be there to support you, but I had to get away before I hurt the ones I loved the most. I hope Tristan was able to stand in my place. See you soon.*

P.S. Don't worry how I see you. Just know that I'm always watching.

F.

Me: *Where are you?*

The number is out of service is what I immediately got back, pissing me off all over again. I slid my phone back in my pocket and focused on my brother. Me and my brother started catching up because I knew that the moment this burial was over, my brother was going back to that cage. At least he didn't have a long time left. Seeing my brother was the best thing about today.

RUBEE

These last couple of weeks had been crazy since Taiwan's parents had been killed at the hands of Romero. My cousin had everybody and everything locked down like it was Fort Knox. Nobody in his family could move two feet without him knowing. Kade didn't want me and Raylee staying over at the house by ourselves, so we had been staying with him. He hadn't even been going to work. He had been working from the house, and I couldn't say that I didn't enjoy it. Even though we had been here with each other, he hadn't gotten on my nerves yet. If this was Bash, I would have been wanting to jump from the second story window. Raylee had taken to Kade really well. She hadn't even asked about her daddy again since the time she told Kade that he was going to be with us until her dad get back.

"What are you thinking about, babe?" Kade whispered.

He whispered because Raylee was sleeping in between us. Over in the middle of the night, she came and got in the bed with us. The sun was shining bright through the curtains, but she was still sleeping. I was going to pull myself out of bed to make all of us some breakfast soon.

"How I been around you for the last few weeks and I'm not tired of you yet. I really love being around you, Kade. Do you think that we would work being in a relationship?" I turned to look at him, and he was already looking at me.

"Serious question. Why wouldn't we work?"

"I can't get out of my own head, honestly. I'm just barely getting two thousand followers on my style page, and—"

"Who won the race? The tortoise or the hare?"

"Kade…" I whined.

"No. Slow and steady won the race. Rubee, as long as you are busting your ass every day, I'm going to be cheering and supporting you. If you wanted to take a break, I would support that. Get out of your own head because I don't give a damn about none of that. You and baby girl make me happy, and as long y'all will have me, I'm going to be here. I don't know how many times I have to tell you that," he said.

I tried to respond, but my stomach started feeling queasy, and my mouth started getting watery. I inflated my stomach and then pulled it back in, just to see if I had to throw up. It was a weird thing I used to do to see if I had to throw up. If I inflated my stomach as far as it could go, and then held it back in, the throw-up would come right up. I did it again, and soon as I pulled my stomach back in, I felt the vomit coming up. I rushed into the bathroom, fell to the floor, and started puking.

When I was done puking, I threw my head back and groaned because I already knew what it was. The same thing happened when I was pregnant with Raylee. I started to cry because I didn't know what the hell I was going to do with another baby.

Kade appeared at the door. "I suppose I'm about to be a father."

I nodded my head and tears slid slowly down my eyes. "I didn't trap you, if that's what you're thinking, Kade."

"You already being defensive, Rubee. I knew what I was doing by nutting in you. You let that fuck nigga get all in your head and shit. I'm not him, Rubee. I want you. I want this child. I want Ray. Do you need a ring or something to prove it?"

"A ring? Like an engagement ring?" I piped up.

"Hell yeah."

"I mean, not if you are going to give me the ring just because I'm pregnant with your baby."

"Nah. You about to make me mad, so I'm going to go in the kitchen and make us some breakfast while you sit here and contemplate on whether you're going to stop acting crazy or not," Kade said and left me on the bathroom floor.

Moments later, Raylee dragged herself in the bathroom. I flushed the toilet before she could see the throw-up in there.

"Good morning, Ray Ray," I spoke to her.

"Good morning, Mommy," she spoke back. "I have to use the bathroom."

I moved out of her way, and she got on the toilet and started using it. While she was using the bathroom, I started brushing my teeth to get this bad taste out of my mouth. While I was brushing my teeth, I kept looking at my stomach since I had on a sports bra. Was I ready for my stomach to get big again? Was I ready to gain all the weight back? Most importantly, was I ready to be a mom again? I said I wanted to get married before I got pregnant again, but I wasn't doing too much to not get pregnant. I wonder what my aunt, uncle, and cousins were going to say.

After Ray got finished using the bathroom, she washed her hands and then started brushing her teeth. After we both finished washing our faces, we went in the kitchen, and Kade was in the middle of cooking breakfast.

"Got anything for me to cut?" Raylee asked Kade.

"No, ma'am. I don't have anything. Maybe later on," Kade told her.

I shook my head because Kade started something that he was going to have to keep up. I just hoped that Raylee didn't develop no knife habit like I have. I moved about the kitchen to set the table for us three. Once Kade was done cooking, he fixed our plates for us. We said grace and we started eating.

"So have you decided which school you liked?" Kade asked me.

"The one with the magic board," Raylee said. "I liked that school, Mom."

BIANCA JONES

I liked St. Mary's as well. They had longer school days than most kids, and they had after school programs for students as well. The school went all the way to the twelfth grade, and they had 100 percent graduation rate. The college completion rate was good as well. The interviewees loved Raylee. I also loved that it was very diverse as well. The one thing I hated was that they didn't have any sports.

"Then there it is. That's where she'll be attending school. We can fill out the paperwork tonight," Kade said.

"What if she wants to play sports one day?" I asked Kade.

"Well, they have all types of AAU sports during the summer, but we can cross that bridge when we get to it. She's going to look so cute in her little uniform."

"I'll pay for the uniforms," I blurted out. "I can't let you do everything."

"Hush."

Before I could respond, my phone started ringing. It was an unknown number. I didn't normally answer these types of calls, and against my better judgement, I answered the phone.

"Hello."

"Rubee, can I speak to my daughter?"

My nostrils immediately started to flare, alarming Kade, and he was immediately by my side. He snatched the phone right out of my hand before I could curse his ass out. Kade walked out of the kitchen, so I don't know what was said, and I didn't have a desire to know. I couldn't believe that he had the nerve to call me.

Moments later, Kade came back in the kitchen and handed me my phone.

"What did you say?"

"Told him if he ever called that phone again, I was going to be the one to put something hot in between his eyes. Matter of fact, you need to get your number changed so he can't get in contact with you anymore."

"Say no more, Daddy Kade."

"Aight, don't play with me, woman," he said and winked at me.

I could get used to being with Kade.

ROMERO

ONE WEEK LATER

I knew that my baby was furious with me for having her parents killed, but all of this could have been avoided had she just bought her ass back to me. The guards that were supposed to be watching their home got caught off guard, which made it even easier. Hearing her cry on the phone three weeks ago hurt me to my core because I knew that she would never come back to me without being forced to now. It was crazy how she was hating me, but she didn't hate the killer that she was sleeping with. The other day, I tried to have her brother knocked off, but it turns out they moved him to solitary confinement and they had him heavily guarded in there. That damn Bailey family was not to be fucked with I see.

I was still over here in Chicago, waiting on Frank to make his next move. Even a man of my stature was getting a little worried because, for the last few weeks, he had been quiet... too damn quiet. After I had Taiwan's parents knocked off, I was expecting to get a video of my son's head being chopped off, but I didn't get it. Since I couldn't get to Tristan, I had to plan my next move carefully, because they all had their families locked down tight. I just had to wait until one of them got caught slipping.

After breakfast, I sat on the balcony and had me a cigar. I was enjoying the nice breeze until my phone started ringing, and it was my brother. I took a deep breath because I knew that he was calling me with some shit about my damn daddy.

"Yeah," I said when I picked up the phone.

"What the fuck have you gotten us into, Romero!" Ralph hollered into the phone.

"What are you talking about, Ralph? I've been over here in Chicago where your father told me I needed to stay, so what are you talking about?" I asked as I thumped the ashes off my cigar.

"Three of our warehouses are gone, Romero. Three whole warehouses are gone. Five of our restaurants are gone. Five."

My body stilled. My mouth opened, but I couldn't say anything. A lump grew in my throat, and I couldn't fix my mouth to ask what he meant by them being *gone*.

"Ralph... explain."

"The warehouse where our weapons were held. Gone. Up in flames. Eighty of our workers were in there. The warehouse with the new drugs that we were getting ready to get put out into the streets next week. Gone. A hundred and fifty of our workers were in there. Olive Street... is up in flames," Ralph spoke.

"Olive Street? Is—"

"UNC! We have to get home, now! Fuck that moolie and his family!" Emmanuel came out on the balcony and shouted.

He showed me his phone with the local news from back home. My phone almost slipped out of my hand when I looked at the aerial view of the city. Different helicopters were in the sky, and it looked like a terrorist had attacked our city.

"Romero!" my brother yelled into the phone, getting my attention. "All of this is your fucking fault. All of it."

"Where is Dad? Where is Ricardo?"

"DEAD! They are DEAD! Romero! They were on their way into one of the restaurants to pick up the money when... oh my fucking... all of this over that black bitch! If I ever see you again, Romero, you're going to be fucking dead!"

"How the fuck are you blaming this on me? We had enemies, Ralph."

"Enemies that would have never done the shit that just went on tonight. If that dude you went to war with don't kill you first, I'm going to do it my goddamn self," Ralph spat before he hung up the phone.

I eased the phone out of my hand and back into my pocket.

"Fuck! I can't get in contact with my dad," Emmanuel said. "What did Uncle Ralph say? Is my dad with them? Where is grandpa?"

"Ricardo and your grandfather were going to pick up the money from..." I said and paused.

"No..." Emmanuel said and backed away from me. "No... You are not going to tell me that... that... that..." He stuttered and swallowed. "You're not going to tell me that my dad and my grandfather is dead at the hands of... hands of..." He fell to his knees and started puking.

My head felt like two elephants were stomping on it. I got up and walked back into the room and sat on the couch. Everyone was looking at me for direction, but at the moment, I didn't know anything but to head back to Italy and give Frank exactly what he wanted. Just as I was getting ready to speak, the flat screen in the room automatically cut on, getting everybody's attention. It was a whole bunch of static before something came up.

My teeth automatically started grinding when I saw Frank come on the screen, sitting in my fucking office, petting Taiwan's dogs! He waved at the camera and then smiled.

"Italy's technology is undefeated, would you agree? I'm talking to you in Chicago, while I'm in Italy. Damn. Did you like the fireworks? I assume you did since you bombed my girlfriend's parents' house."

"How the fuck did you get into my home!" I shouted. "Angel, Flash! Attack!" I ordered the dogs, but they didn't do anything.

"Oh please!" Frank waved me off and chuckled. "We've been bonding for the last few hours."

"Where is my wife? Where are my sons and my nephew? You piece of shit! You've killed hundreds of innocent people tonight!"

"Now, I wouldn't call anyone names, Romero," he said and got up and walked out into the hallway.

He was definitely in my home because that was my hundred-thousand-dollar pillow soft carpet that had blood stains all over it. He finally walked into the bedroom that I shared with Essie. He pointed the camera toward the bed, and Essie was tied up, along with her boyfriend, Brandon, and my two sons, Romero Jr. and Marco. Romero Jr. and Marco looked as if they had been beaten halfway to death. They were all tied to the headboard with tape over their mouths.

Frank jumped on the bed and yelled, "Family timeeee!" He smiled in the camera while my family looked completely afraid in the back.

I caved. "What do you want?"

I would never be the same if I watched him kill my family.

"Oohhhhh, nowwwww it's what I want? When I *told* you what I wanted the first time, you ignored it. You *completely* ignored it. Even after I *showed* you what I was about the first time, you still ignored it, but now that I have the wife that you were going to leave for *my* girl, her boyfriend, and your sons, now, it's what I want. I want Taiwan's parents' heads back on their shoulders, but that's not going to happen, is it? I want my girl to be able to sleep good at night, but that's not going to happen is it? There is a list of things that I want."

I picked up the phone to call Ralph to tell him to get to my home, but Frank cocked his gun and put it to Brandon's head.

POW!

He pulled the trigger before I could even beg for the boy's life. He held his head back and inhaled sharply.

"I love the smell of fresh blood," he said and smiled. "Put the phone down!" he ordered me. "The next bullet will be in your wife's neck, and you're going to have to watch her bleed out. Don't fuck with me."

"What do you want? Money? You can have it all. Please don't kill the only people I have left. You killed my brother and my father. I have no one left."

"Oh, yes you do! You have one brother left that wants to kill you as much as I do," he replied. "And oh, I don't want your money. It is of no use to me. I have my own. I want your life, Romero. I won't be able to sleep knowing that you are still breathing, and oh, can you hurry up and get here because I haven't had no pussy in three weeks, and I need to get home to my girl so I can bust this load in her."

My jaws clenched. My blood was boiling. I couldn't wait to kill him. He thought this shit was a fucking joke. I was definitely going to kill him before he killed me.

"Oh, let me put some fire behind you," he said.

He cocked the gun again, and shot Essie, Marco, and Romero Jr. He blew a kiss into the camera and it went dead.

For the first time in my life, I had fucked with someone more diabolical than me.

FRANK

The day I walked away from Mayhem and Taiwan, I went to my house, grabbed a few things that I needed, and then I chartered a jet to Italy. No lie, it was cool as fuck over here though, and the food was good. I could see why Taiwan loved it over here. I was lucky that Emmanuel still hadn't found the tracker nor the listening device, so they were giving me mostly everything that I needed, but I got everything else from Miguel. I dragged him and his cousin over here on the jet as well. It was so easy to set they asses up, and I was loving every minute of it. I could honestly say that I felt bad for killing Essie because I didn't kill women, but Romero didn't exercise his morals when he killed Taiwan's mom, so I did the same thing. It was his fault that I had turned this way.

When I made it back to the place I was staying, Miguel was sleep against the headboard. I was still keeping his ass tied up because I didn't trust him, but at least I was feeding him every day now, so he'd better be grateful. I was still on the fence on whether I wanted to let him go or not. I would know for sure what I wanted to do by the time I got on the jet to go back home. I kicked my shoes off and grabbed my iPad. I pressed a few buttons on the screen, and I smiled when she came on the screen. She was on her knees and praying. She had been

AN INSANE LOVE 3

doing that about five times a day, and I appreciated it because I needed all the prayers that I could get. I wanted to call her, but I needed to stay focused.

"God, please protect Frank. Please, God. Wherever he is, please keep him covered in your blood. Lord, when he makes it back to me, I promise I'll tell him that I love him. I'll protect him. I know that he's troubled, but it's nothing that real love can't fix. God. I'll tell him that I forgive him for almost twisting my arm off. If you bring him back to me, I promise to help You take care of him. Lord, I won't be able to do any of this without You. Please protect Mayhem too. I know he's going to where Frank is, but he didn't want to tell me. Please keep them covered, Lord. I don't want to live without Frank being in my life, and I know Olena would die if something happened to Mayhem. In Jesus name, I pray, Amen," Taiwan prayed.

"Amen," I whispered.

My parents really did a number on me. They used to piss me off so bad, doing shit to me that no child should go through, that when I got mad, I would black out. When I blacked out, I either whooped somebody's ass or I would just sit still and stare. Sometimes I could come out of myself, but most times, I had to be restrained. Luckily, since I'd been older, I'd only blacked out around Mayhem, and he knew to cut my air supply off to bring me out of the trance. I knew for a fact I was much stronger when I blacked out, and that was why I almost broke Taiwan's arm. That shit made me feel so bad. Everything was my fucking parents' fault. All of this shit. I didn't want to watch Taiwan cry, so I turned off the iPad and placed it on the table.

There was one knock on the door.

A small pause.

Then two quick knocks.

A long pause.

Then three quick knocks.

I got up and walked over to the door because I knew that it was Mayhem because that had always been our secret knock. When I opened the door, it was him and that white Fed bitch, Alicia. I told Mayhem to bring her because I remembered Taiwan mentioned that she wanted to bust him, and she would let Tristan out early. That was the only reason I invited her as well, because I was going to make sure that she kept her promise. Tristan was all the family that she had left, and plus, it was time for that nigga to come out of there anyway. He had been in there forever for something that any nigga would have done for their sister.

I dapped Mayhem up and let them in the room. They both were looking around in shock because the outside of this place didn't look shit like the inside, and that was why I liked it.

"It doesn't look like you need me," Alicia said.

"I don't. I just wanted you to bust his ass so you can get Tristan out of jail like you promised my girl. Other than that, we ain't got shit to talk about," I snapped.

I noticed the tension between her and Mayhem, but I ignored it. I knew that he hated police just as much as I did.

"Is there a reason why this young man is tied to the headboard?" Alicia asked and placed her hand on Miguel's neck, making him jump awake, prompting her to jump back.

"Did you miss the last part of that sentence where I said other than that, we ain't got shit to talk about? Don't come up in here asking questions about shit, or I'll send your ass back to Chicago."

She looked at me and then gave me a tight-lipped smile. "I looked you up. Why you fifty and working on a case like this?"

"Oh, I can talk now?" she asked.

"Bitch," I hissed.

"This is supposed to be my last case, and I was going to retire so I can spend time with my kids and grandkids."

"Oh. You the first white person I seen that hadn't aged like milk. You got some good moisturizer."

I laughed, but she didn't see nothing funny.

"Well, let's get some rest. We gotta be well prepared. They are on their way back over here. I'm about to murk this nigga, close her case, and then go back home to my girl."

"What about him?" Mayhem asked.

"I don't know yet. He ain't been on no crazy shit, and he been really helpful, so we'll see. He said he got a mom down in Florida, but I'll see."

The Next Night

I have hurt a lot of people in my lifetime, so I didn't even know if God be listening to me or if He sent my prayers right to the spam folder, but I'd been saying a small prayer all day. This was the biggest mission that I had ever taken on in my life. For some odd reason, I had a few jitter bugs in my stomach, but I also felt completely safe and covered. I felt that if I died tonight, I wouldn't die in vain, and my girl would forever be safe.

"You ready?" Mayhem asked me.

We were standing outside where I had been staying for the last few weeks, about to get in a van. It was a plain black van that looked just like the vans that some of the Santiago men rode in. Getting these niggas was going to be too easy. I already knew their location because I had tracked Emmanuel's tracker.

"You know I'm always ready, bruh. Before we get in this van, I want to offer you the opportunity to go back home and be with the girls and the kids. Big bro, you have risked your life for me on more than one occasion, and I can't ask—"

"Aye! Tell me this shit when we get back to Chi Town. We are going to make it back home, aight," Mayhem said and pulled me into a brotherly hug. "This shit about to go down in history."

I opened the back door, and Mayhem got in the back, along with a few of our most trusted guys and some of Alicia's team that she had called. She promised that when she does her report, me, Mayhem, and our organization will be left out of it, and as much as I didn't want to,

I was going to hold this white bitch to her word. After I closed Mayhem in, I got in the front with Alicia at the wheel. She pulled off pretty slow, and we headed toward the warehouse.

"I'm going to tell you when to stop," I told her.

"Where are you from?" she asked me.

"No disrespect, but now ain't the time for formalities," I told her.

"Ma-Frank, when all of this is over, I need to talk to you about something. Maybe over dinner or something. Taiwan is welcome to come along too," she said.

"Aye! Shut the fuck up! He needs to be focused," Mayhem shouted from the back.

She put her lips together and stared ahead. Me and this lady had nothing in common, so there was nothing that she needed to speak to me about. Once she got eighty yards away from the warehouse, I told her to stop. I put my special made binoculars up to my eyes to see how many men were there walking around outside. I knew that they probably had beefed up security because that was the last warehouse they had left, and that one held their drugs. If I was a thief, I would take their drugs once I was finished knocking their asses off, but I ain't want to leave them down bad like that.

"Mayhem, hand me my rifle."

There were three dudes standing outside the gate. After I got my rifle from Mayhem, I started putting it together.

"I figured that if I can hit this bullet off that metal thing, I can take the first two guys out, and then I can easily take the other guy out," I said to myself.

"You can do that?" Alicia asked surprisingly.

"I wasn't talking to you, but yeah, I can. Hold these binoculars and watch me work."

I let the window down and got out the van. I set the handle of the rifle on the window, and then leaned over to where I could see out of the scope. I had my eyes on them, and I smiled because they were really in the perfect position. The guy on the far right turned around and walked away from the other two guys. I aimed the gun toward the metal thing and eased my finger down on the trigger.

Pow!

The bullet ricocheted off the metal things and the bullet went through both of the guys heads. It really paid to have money to get things that other people couldn't get. The other guy tried to take off running, but I got him right in the back of the head. I smiled to myself and then got back in the van.

"Wow. That's impressive," Alicia said.

I didn't say anything, but I told her to drive. After we made it to the gates, I got out, and went into the guard station and opened the gates. I grabbed a radio off one of the dead men before we pulled into the gates. I opened my iPad and tapped on the screen for a few seconds before I hacked into their cameras. There were no men by the front door like it should have been, and there were no men at the back door. There were men upstairs bagging up the drugs, and men downstairs playing cars. If I walked into the front door, no one would fucking notice. I spotted Romero upstairs in an office, along with three men and his big ass nephew. It looked like over the weeks, his ass gained all the weight back he'd lost, plus more.

"Tony, who was that you just let in the gates?" Romero's voice came through the radio.

"I'm about to kill the cameras and the lights in one minute," I announced to the people in the van.

"Tony, do you copy? My uncle asked you who did you let in the gates?" Emmanuel asked.

"I'm going to go through the front door with a couple of men, and the rest of y'all going around back. Alicia, you stay your ass out here in this van."

"No! I can help."

"Nah, we need you out here in case we need to peel out real fast, aight," I told her.

She looked like she had an attitude, but she stayed her ass in the van when everybody got out. I made sure my vest was tight, and I had extra clips in reach. I made sure everybody was straight before I sent them around to the back door.

As soon as I got to the door, I pressed the button on the radio and said, "Your worst nightmare."

I killed the cameras and the lights. I burst into the front door and immediately started ducking behind shit. The guys that came through the front door with me hit the floor once we heard the first exchange of gunfire. The warehouse was pitch black with the exception of the few lights that came on from the backup generator.

Pow! Pow! Pow! Pow!

Tat-tat-tat-tat-tat-tat

Pow! Pow! Pow!

Tat-tat-tat-tat

There was a lot of exchange of gunfire. I bear walked across the room until I got behind a flipped over table, while the other guys went the other way. Whoever was shooting at me was lighting the table up.

Pow! Pow! Pow!

I stood up and let off three shots and took that nigga out, but I took one in the chest. I ducked back behind the table and rubbed the place where I was shot.

I grimaced. "Shit."

The radio that I had clipped to my vest started going off.

"You fucked with the right one. You come on my turf, thinking that you are going to kill me, huh?" Romero said into the radio.

I pushed the button. "I don't *think* shit. I know."

The gunfire simmered down for a second, and I peeked over the table just in time to see another guy reloading his clip, and I had a chance to take his ass out. Everybody on the bottom floor was dead or hiding really well. I crept up the stairs and hid behind a wall and pressed the radio.

"Come out, you bitch! It's just me and you now! Come out and fight me like a real man," I said.

He chuckled into the radio. "Son, don't let this old age fool you."

I peeked out from behind the wall, and I saw Mayhem, and my heart damn near stopped. I ain't know if my boy was alive or dead, but seeing him made me let out sigh. He held his thumb up and then down, basically asking me if I was hurt, and I held my thumb up. I was hurt, but not deadly hurt. I was just going to have a bad ass bruise from the bullet.

I pressed the button on the radio. "Come downstairs and let's go. No weapons. I bet you can't fuck with me. You want Taiwan? Fight me for her."

He chuckled again but didn't say anything. Three men eased out of one of the rooms, and both me and Mayhem lit they asses up. Mayhem ran down the hallway to me and got on the other side of the wall.

"You got hit?" I asked him.

"A couple times on the side, but I'm good," he whispered.

Tat-tat-tat-tat-tat-tat-tat-tat

These niggas started shooting through the walls, and I dived off the banister, pulling Mayhem with me. Mayhem landed on his back, knocking the wind out of him, and I tried to land on my feet, but I ended up twisting my fucking ankle. I was laying on my back in the egg position, trying to check on my ankle, but the shit was hurting too bad. I noticed that Mayhem was on his back, trying to breathe. Getting the wind knocked out of you wasn't no joke.

"Bro... come on, breathe. You aight," I said and slapped his face a couple of times.

After a few moments, Mayhem got his breathing under control.

"You straight, bro?" I asked him.

"Yeah, are you?"

"Hell nah. My ankle is fucked up. It's not broken because the pain would be much worse than it is now. Come on, you gotta help me out of here," I said to him.

Mayhem stood up and pulled me to my feet. I could barely put pressure on it before wincing in pain. The minute we made it to the door, we heard someone start talking behind us.

"Leaving so soon."

We turned around to see Romero and Emmanuel standing there, they both had guns pointed on us.

"Drop him!" Romero ordered Mayhem.

He didn't do it right away, and they both cocked their guns. I took my arm away from Mayhem's neck, and instead of him dropping me, he didn't, so he literally had me by my waist.

"Nah, I ain't letting my guy go. You gon' have to shoot us both," Mayhem growled.

Romero started taking off his suit jacket. "You wanted a fight, so I'm about to give you one. Come on. Surely that ankle not bothering a strong man like you," Romero taunted me.

I started taking off my vest because the extra weight was going to be holding me back.

"What are you doing?" Mayhem whispered.

"I gotta do this."

Mayhem let me go, and I limped as best as I could toward him. He placed his gun on the ground, and I did the same thing. I looked at Mayhem, and he had both of his guns in his hands, ready to shoot, and Emmanuel was still holding his gun. Romero got in his fight stance, and I held my hands up. At that very moment, I could hear my dad's voice.

Chaz, focus!

I can't hit you if you don't let me!

Romero swung at me, but I ducked out of the way quickly, but I fell because of my ankle. I jumped back up, and I could feel my adrenaline start to flow, and I was able to apply just a little pressure. Romero got back in his fighting stance.

Come on, Chaz!

Fucking hit me!

Bam! Bam!

I hit Romero twice and moved back because he tried to counter my swing but missed.

Swinging and missing tires them out, Chaz.

Focus!

Bam! Bam! Bam!

Romero three pieced my ass really quick, and I could feel my nose start to bleed and my eye start swelling. He had on some big rings on his hand. Old man hit hard. I couldn't lie about that.

AN INSANE LOVE 3

"Oh yeah, that's all you got? You pack quite a punch," I taunted him.

I got back in my fighting stance.

Focus, Chaz. Focus.

Bam! Bam! Bam! Bam!

I hit Romero with a combination of two right hooks and two left hooks to his body, making him double over. It took all the strength I had to knee him in his face, before my ankle gave out on me, and I fell with him in my arms. I had him in a headlock, and he kept trying to get loose.

"Old fucking man! Old fucking man! You fucked with the right fucking family! All you had to do was leave us the fuck alone," I growled.

He kicked my ankle, and I yelled out in agony and let him go and scooted back so I could hurry up and get on my feet. Before I could get up, Romero stomped on my ankle.

Wam!

He kicked me in my side.

"She was my fucking bitch!" he growled.

Wam!

"You not so mouthy now are you?"

Wam!

"You killed my wife!"

Wam!

"Frank, get up!" Mayhem shouted. "Focus, Frank! Get up!"

Wam!

He raised his foot and stomped me in my chest, and I grabbed his ankle, twisting it around, making Romero fall on his face. I scooted away from him because it was getting hard for me to breathe because of how hard he was kicking me in my ribs. I knew a lot of them were broken. I looked at Emmanuel, and he pointed his gun at me, cocked it, and before I could roll out of the way of the gun, he pulled the trigger and shot me in my stomach. I laid back and held my hand on the bullet wound and tried to control my bleeding.

POW! POW! POW!

Emmanuel went down to the ground, and Mayhem was at my side. "DROP IT! NOW!"

Romero was standing over me with a gun pointed down at me.

"If you don't drop your weapons now, I'm going to shoot him again."

"Drop… drop… drop it, bro," I stuttered.

"I ain't dropping shit!" Mayhem shouted and then looked up at Romero.

Romero cocked his gun.

"You heard him. Drop it."

Mayhem eased the guns down, and Romero kicked them away.

"Look at you. Look at you. Look at you now. How you think Taiwan would feel knowing that you over here and died a gruesome death, huh?"

"That I died for her, bitch. Do it. Finish it," I taunted him.

He cocked the gun and then he suddenly fell to his knees with a bullet wound in his head. Mayhem looked around and then focused back on me.

"Frank… hold on. Frank. Please hold on," Mayhem said and helped me hold the wound.

I started to spit up blood. I could feel myself start to suffocate.

"I lo-lo-love you," I stuttered out.

With tears falling from Mayhem's eyes, he said, "Tell me that shit when we get back. Tell me that shit when we get back to Chi-Town."

I let out a small laugh. "Yo-yo-you-cry-cry baby bitch."

"ALICIA!" Mayhem shouted out, and that was the last thing I heard.

Two weeks later

AN INSANE LOVE 3

My left eye fluttered opened, and it was fuzzy. I closed my eye again and opened it again. I could see that Mayhem was on one side of my bed and Alicia was on the other side. They were whispering loudly.

"No, you ain't telling him shit.."

"He has the right to know!"

"No! You will not tell him shit. He's... we've been through enough."

I tried to cough, and that shit hurt like hell. Whatever was in my mouth, I started pulling on it because I felt like I was suffocating again. It hurt too bad to keep yanking on it, so I stopped.

"Frank." Mayhem called my name. "Hold on. Let me get the doctor."

Moments later, the doctor rushed into the room and started flashing lights in my eyes.

"Mr. Wade, my name is Dr. Moore. I am going to take this tube out of your throat. It's going to be uncomfortable for a few seconds," he said, and I slightly nodded my head.

It took him a moment before he pulled whatever he had to pull out of my throat, and I instantly felt better.

"The nurse is going to go get you something to drink, okay. I'll be in to talk to you after you've had a couple of glasses of water, okay?"

I nodded my head, and they both left my face. Mayhem came over to me and look at me.

"Bitch," I whispered.

Mayhem laughed. "You'll be back to yourself in no time. You've been in a coma for the last couple of weeks. You're back in Chicago, though. Once they got you stable enough in Italy, we brought you back over here. Romero is no longer a problem."

"Who—"

"Shit, I don't know. The shot came out of nowhere. Alicia said she ain't do it."

I closed my eyes and shook my head because I couldn't believe it. I didn't want to get my hopes up, but if what I was thinking was true, then I had so many mixed feelings.

My parents are back.

KADE

Both me and Rubee were on pins and needles, sitting in this doctor's office. With everything that had been going on with Taiwan's parents getting murdered, Frank and Mayhem damn near getting themselves killed over in Italy, and Bash and Alex going missing, we didn't want to seem insensitive by announcing the pregnancy when we first found out. Since we were at our first official appointment, I could barely contain my excitement. I would get to get ultrasounds, hear the heartbeat, or something. I didn't know how this shit worked. Rubee kept trying to tell me how everything worked, but I was just too damn excited to settle down and listen.

"I'm going to tell my aunt and uncle first. I already know that my mom and dad is going to trip and think that I'm wasting my life away by continuing to have kids. You should have heard how they scolded me when I first got pregnant with Ray. They stressed me out so bad. That's probably why I went into labor early," Rubee turned to me and said.

"But see, you in a different situation now, bae. You got a nigga that's going to take care of you throughout everything. You got a nigga that's going to ride for you regardless. You got a nigga that got you pregnant on purpose and is ready to be a father," I assured her.

"You sure?"

"Hell yeah."

I said hell yeah, but the same night after I found out, I couldn't help but to think about what type of father I would be. Would I be strict? Would I be overprotective? Would I hover over them daily? I mean, I knew what type of father I was not going to be, and that was like Kason Lewis. I already had the blueprint of what not to be. The next morning, Rubee assured me that I would be a great father because I was a great person in general.

"Bailey…" The lady called out Rubee's name.

"We gon' have to do something about that shit," I mumbled and helped her up out of her seat.

"Do something about what?" she asked me.

"That 'Bailey' shit. I like the sound of Rubee Lewis. Do you?"

I could tell that her heart stilled when I said it, and she smiled.

"All you have to do is ask me. Are you sure you ready to be married?"

"Been ready," I said and kissed her forehead.

Nine weeks pregnant. Rubee was nine weeks pregnant. Her stomach didn't even have a pudge or nothing, and it worried me that our baby wasn't growing. Rubee told me she gained only ten pounds with Raylee because she didn't have a chance to get really big with her because Raylee was premature. The doctor said that everything looked good, and one day we were going to wake up and wonder where her stomach came from. We heard the baby's heartbeat, and a real nigga had tears in his eyes. I never thought that I would be a father. I swear I thought that I was going to be forty with a newborn baby. A nigga thought that he was going to be dragging an oxygen tank to his kid's preschool graduation.

Me and Rubee were on our way to her aunt and uncle's house, holding hands. Raylee was at Mayhem's house playing with the twins. It actually felt good to be able to roam around without security up our asses. My phone rang, and the caller ID said 'Unknown'. Rubee looked at me with a crazy look on her face. I knew it wasn't nobody but my daddy. We hadn't talked in a long ass time.

"Answer it," she said.

I picked it up, and the operator told me it was my daddy calling and asked if I wanted to accept the charges.

"Son... is everybody okay?" he asked me.

"Yes. Everybody is fine. I'm fine."

"See, that's why I didn't want that fucking family in our lives. They got my children's lives in danger because of a damn cartel." Kason huffed.

"Dad, chill. We are fine. Security was so tight that we could barely go to the bathroom."

"That don't matter. You shouldn't have been in that situation to begin with. Where are you now?"

"Dad. Please don't forget your part in this, aight? Your part in this is also the reason why you're in prison for the rest of your life."

I could feel myself getting a headache, and I wasn't about to let my dad ruin this day for me.

"Have you talked to your sisters?"

"I always talk to them."

"Can you convince them to come see me? I really miss my daughters, son. I haven't seen Kalena in years. I know she's grown now. I write her, and she don't even write me back."

"Yeah, she's in college, doing her thing. Loving it. I'll talk to her about it, but I can't make Kam come see you because..." I paused when I looked over at Rubee smiling down at her phone like the only person besides her daughter that makes her smile that way isn't sitting next to her.

AN INSANE LOVE 3

"Girl, you about to get your ass kicked up out of here. *Ejecto seato, cuz!*" I mimicked Tyrese from *2 Fast 2 Furious*.

"Nigga, you is on the phone, not paying me no attention, so I'm on here talking to somebody that wanna give me some attention."

"Girl... I'll run this damn car into the median and kill us both. Who the fuck you talking to?" I hissed.

"You ain't crazy," she snapped.

I snatched the phone out of her hand and looked at the screen. It was a picture of our daughter smiling with icing on her face along with her cousins. I felt like shit, so I gave her back her phone and didn't even look at her.

"Yeah, look at you," she said and laughed.

"Son, who is that you're talking to?"

"My fiancée, Rubee... Bailey. We are on the way to Korupt's house to tell him that another baby is coming soon."

"Your fiancée? Bailey? Pregnant? What is it with them damn Baileys? Why can't y'all stay the fuck away from them? They ruined our damn lives."

"Listen, old man! You got me—"

Snap. Snap.

I cut Rubee off because she was getting ready to go ham on my pops, and she rolled her eyes and looked out the window. I loved and hated that attitude. She probably needed some dick, and I was going to supply her with it as soon as we get back to the house.

"Dad, I'm going to let you go. Call me back in a few weeks. I'd been have talked to Kalena by then," I said and hung up the phone.

"Jail still ain't changed him, man," I said to Rubee.

She already knew the story just like everybody else did, so it didn't make no sense in going over it again. I asked Kalena last year around Christmas time if she wanted to go see our dad, but she said no. She said that she wasn't ready to go see him, and I couldn't blame her. For the first year or so after everything went down, I suggested therapy and shit because I ain't want her to keep her feelings bottled up, but she convinced me that she was fine. I paid attention to her behavior, and it hadn't changed. She was still her happy-go-lucky self.

Twenty minutes later, we pulled up to Angela and Korupt's house and parked. I got out the car and then helped her out and walked up to the door. I knocked on the door, and moments later, the door opened, and Korupt stared at us.

"Why y'all standing here looking like one of those stock pictures in the frames at Walmart?" he asked, and then looked at me and then down at Rubee. "Aw, hell naw. You better not be coming over here to tell me that you pregnant, Rubee."

"Uncle…"

"ANGELA!" he called out to his wife.

"Whatttt?" she said, coming up to the door. "Lord, why you standing there looking crazy? Please don't tell me you pregnant, because I just got off the phone with your mama telling her that she was only dreaming of fish because she was craving it."

"Auntie…" Rubee said and paused.

"And let me guess, she pregnant from you?" Korupt asked while looking me up and down.

Contrary to popular belief, I had never seen the mean side of Paxton like Malice and Mayhem said he has. Even with the shit going on with my dad and him, I never saw the mean side of him. Looking at him standing here with his nostrils flaring, I didn't know what he was about to do. Paxton was tall and stocky as fuck. This nigga had me by like three inches in height and about sixty pounds in weight, but the shit was all muscle. I only prayed that I looked half as good as him when I get older. I was sure I'd be able to go toe to toe with him if he hit me and knocked me off these steps, but I didn't want to change the dynamics of our family if I had to whoop Korupt's ass… or try to anyway.

"Yeah, but we are going to get through this. Just invite me in so we can talk."

He continued to stare at me for another three minutes before he moved away from the door and let us in. We sat at the dining room table, and I was going to let them speak first. Twenty minutes later, neither of them had said anything. It was like we were just sitting here having a stare down, but I couldn't take it anymore.

"I know y'all mad…"

"Mad? I'm way past mad. Rubee is only twenty-five years old, about to have her second child with a second baby daddy. She doesn't have a job, and she ain't never worked before in her life. The first baby daddy is a piece of—"

"Hold on, Korupt. I respect you a great deal, but I'm not going to let you talk about her like she's some bum, when she's not. Rubee does have a job. She's my stylist and takes my photos. She wants to be a stylist and a photographer, so she's going to start with me. Yes, she gets paid with direct deposit and will have a W2 at the end of the year. She already has two thousand followers on her Instagram page. I always shout her out on my work pages, so she could get more exposure."

I had to calm down because I didn't want to disrespect a man in his own home, but talking about the mother of my child will always get me hot, and I didn't give a damn who had something to say about it.

"Look, I know you are pissed about Rubee getting pregnant again, but—"

"You're going to let him speak for you like this, Rubee?" Paxton asked.

Rubee opened her mouth to speak, but I held my hand up, and she pursed her lips together. "As I was saying before, I know that both of y'all are pissed that she got pregnant again, but this time around, she's going to have a damn good support system behind her. She's not going to be stressed out, and the baby is going to be raised in a loving environment, along with our other daughter, Raylee. Don't just be mad at her. I share in the blame, because I never used a condom with her. Rubee is going to be a great mom to this one…" I placed my hand on her stomach. "…just like she is to Raylee. If Raylee's smarts ain't an indicator of how smart her mother is, then I don't know what to tell you. Raylee just got into St. Mary's and will be starting there next year, and before you say anything, the tuition will be paid by me. Honestly, if Rubee don't want to ever clock into anything, she doesn't have to, because I'm going to take care of mine."

"All that shit sounds good, but I ain't hear no talk about marrying her. You just want her to be a baby mama?"

"Yes, we have discussed marriage. I don't want to rush her because of what she just went through with her first baby daddy. Whenever she is ready to get married, then that's what's going to happen. I've been wanting to be a husband and a father, and I can't think of no one else to have that with other than my lil' crazy woman, Rubee," I said and looked at her.

Tears were welling up in her eyes, and I could tell that she appreciated me standing up for her. Paxton inhaled and exhaled slowly and grabbed the bridge of his nose. I guess he wasn't expecting me to lay things out on the table for him like that.

"Rubee, do you understand why we are concerned?" Angela asked her.

"Yes, Auntie, but I love Kade."

I whipped my head around to her because although I knew that we both were feeling it, we hadn't said it to each other yet. Hearing her say those words made me want to lean over and plant a sloppy ass kiss on her lips.

"The first time around felt forced. I loved Bash because he is my child's father. We got pregnant, and staying with him felt like the right thing to do. I have always wanted what you two have, Uncle and Auntie. I have always wanted what my parents have. I always wanted to be married with a strong man that could take care of me when the time comes, and that's what I have with Kade. Nothing with Kade feels forced. The way he shows his love for me is… is something that I can barely explain. The way he loves my daughter is something I never expected to find so soon. He really wants the best for me, Uncle and Auntie. I promise. He be checking me when I get rowdy with people, and I no longer walk around with a blade in my cheek. He's taught me ways to channel my anger into something else. He's perfect for me, and I couldn't have asked for a better baby daddy, and yes, I can't wait to marry him."

It got quiet for a moment, and I didn't know what he was about to say.

"So, Paxton, do I have your blessing to marry Rubee?" I asked him.

Angela looked at him, and he looked down at her. I held my breath, waiting for the answer that he was about to give me.

"The age difference?" Paxton asked me. "Those things start to show their hands later in relationships. How I know you won't get tired of Rubee by the time you're thirty-five and both of y'all interests change?"

"Then we are going to work through it. We are going to find a common ground because it ain't no divorce, aight. Me and Rubee are going to be doing this forever. I know marriage ain't peaches and cream, but if we really love each other and are willing to put in the work, we'll be fine."

There was another pause before Paxton said, "Okay."

"Okay, what?" both me and Rubee said at the same time.

"You have my blessing to marry my niece, but you are going to have to fly down to Texas and tell her dad. He's not as understanding as me, so that smart charming shit you just used on me, might not work on him," he said, making me laugh.

I would do whatever I had to do to be with Rubee's beautiful ass. The rest of the afternoon was spent chilling with the older Baileys and listening to them talk about marriage and babies.

TAIWAN

THE NEXT MORNING

My eyes opened at seven this morning like they had been doing for the last six weeks. I dropped to my knees and prayed for Frank like I had been doing since the day after he left me standing in that alleyway. He was out of the hospital, but he was sleeping in the other room because he kept claiming that he wanted to be alone. After he ignored me the first night, I came to the big house and started sleeping in the guest bedroom. I wasn't about to be dealing with his bipolar ass ways.

Frank had been out of the hospital for almost a week, and he still hadn't said much to me, and I hadn't said much to him either. Most of the time, he was doped up on medicine, and the other time, he was sleep. The shot to the stomach and the broken ankle really took a toll on his body, but I was happy that he was alive. Although he took off for weeks to save everybody's life, it still didn't change the fact that I felt a way about him not contacting me. When Mayhem first contacted everybody and said that they had landed back in Chicago but Frank was in a coma, I felt like I couldn't breathe. It felt as if everything around me was caving in. I was thinking how God could snatch my parents away, and now he was about to snatch Frank. I couldn't eat, and I couldn't sleep, and when I finally passed out from starving myself, the family doctor came over and checked me out. Imagine my fucking surprise when Dr. Hawkins told me that I was pregnant. The only person that knew was Olena. He told me that I was going to have to go and get an ultrasound from an OB/GYN, and I was going to go get that today. I didn't know how I was going to tell him since he wasn't talking to me.

Ever since Dr. Hawkins told me that I was pregnant, I had been eating up a storm, and thankfully, I hadn't had any morning sickness. I didn't know why, but I had been pushing on my stomach a lot lately. I didn't know what I was expecting to feel, but nothing had changed since Dr. Hawkins told me. I looked at the time, and only thirty minutes had gone by, and my appointment wasn't until two in the afternoon, so I had time to eat breakfast and take me another nap. I went into the bathroom to wash my face and brush my teeth before going downstairs and being social. After I finished brushing my teeth and washing my face, I put on my robe and went downstairs, and Olena was already in the kitchen feeding Pier's chunky self.

"He's not going to be able to walk if you keep feeding him," I said to her and took him out of her arms.

"You better get ready," she whispered and touched my stomach. "Have you told him yet?"

"Girl, that light bright ass nigga still ain't talking to me, so I'm not going to kiss his ass, girl."

"I think him knowing that he's about to be a father would cheer him up a little. He's been through a lot within the last few weeks. So, just go easy on him a little, okay. Plus, that medicine got him delirious and shit. He'll be fine soon. You know can't no damn gunshot keep a nigga like Frank down."

That made me smile, because Frank was a real soldier.

"So, you want me to come with you?"

"No. I'm a big girl. Maybe I'll show him the thing later today, and maybe he'll talk to me."

Olena took Pier away from me and went back upstairs. I pulled the eggs and veggies out and made me a veggie omelet. I'd been craving peppers a lot; well, anything hot. I knew that the doctor was going to tell me that a lot of hot stuff was not good for the baby. After I finished cooking my omelet, I went upstairs to eat. After I finished eating, I set the plate on the nightstand and laid down. I started scrolling social media since I was back on there, and all the rumors and shit about me had died down. There were a few trolls that would be commenting on my shit about my naked photos and my involvement with my parents' murders, but I would block them. My block list was a mile long. After a few minutes of scrolling social media, I set my alarm clock for noon, placed my phone on the nightstand, and dozed off.

Three hours later...

In my sleep, I could feel my face getting wet. I swatted at my face, but it was getting wetter. The small cries made my eyes shoot open, and I let out a scream when I saw who I was looking at.

"Oh my Goddd! Angel and Flash!" I screamed.

Their tails were wagging a whole lot, and they were jumping all over me. I cried tears of joy because I couldn't believe they were in my face. Angel and Flash always made my days a little bit better. I looked at the door, and I saw Frank leaning against the door. I jumped out of the bed and went to hug him.

"I wish I could jump on you and hug you, Franklin!" I cried and tried to kiss him.

"Nun-uh. You got dog slob on your face," he said and hobbled to the bed to sit down.

He had a cast and a boot on the leg where his ankle was broken.

"Are you in pain?"

"Just a little bit." He groaned.

"You want me to go get your meds?"

"Nah, I'm sick of sleeping and feeling like a zombie. I think I'mma try to thug it out until night time."

"Oh," I said, not knowing what else to say.

"Frank… thanks for this. I've had them since they were puppies, and I thought about them every day."

"I thought that you would like them here. They are some good dogs, but we are going to train them mothafuckas to eat flesh and not no kibbles and bits. They about to be some guard dogs."

"They are my guard dogs. I bet you won't raise your voice at me."

He chuckled. "I'm sure not, and I can't run in that bathroom and lock the door."

"Frank… what you did for me…" I paused.

"Don't worry about it. I'd do it all over again if I had to. Can you shower and come to the guesthouse? I need it…"

"Can we at least talk, Frank?"

"About what?"

"Your mental—"

"I'm still crazy. That's not going to change. Now, get showered and meet me over at the guesthouse in twenty minutes," he said and stood up. "Mayhem said the dogs can't stay in the house because of the kids, but they are welcome to roam free on the property. Don't worry though. I'll get them a dope ass dog house right next to the guesthouse for the time being."

I blew out a sigh of frustration because Frank was always going to be Frank. Closed off.

After I showered and let the dogs out, I walked to the guesthouse. When I walked in the guesthouse, it was pitch black. I walked into the bedroom, and Frank had rose petals all over the bed, and slow jams were playing on the speaker in the corner. He was sitting on the bed in all his naked glory. The bullet wound in his shoulder had completely healed, but there was still a scar. His stomach was patched up really good, and he was lucky as fuck that the bullet missed any vital organs, and he didn't have to wear a shit bag for the rest of his life. His dick was standing up and oozing with pre-cum.

"What you still standing over there for? Bring your beautiful ass over here, ma," he said.

I walked over to him and stood in between his legs. He tugged at my shorts and pulled them down, and I stepped out of them. I didn't have on any panties, so he could dive right in if he wanted to. The way I was feeling right now, if he blew on my clit, I would cum. Frank wrapped his arms around my waist and laid his head on my freshly waxed mound.

"You smell good, shorty. Get on your knees for me."

I eased on my knees, and he grabbed the bottom of my shirt and pulled it over my head. He started massaging my titties and then instructed me to look up at him, because all I could focus on was those shiny ass metal pieces sticking out of the shaft of his dick.

"These titties are juicy as fuck, girl. What the hell were you eating when I was gone? I like this shit though," he said and kept playing with them, making me chuckle.

"Frank, lay back and let me suck your dick, please?"

"Please? You begging to suck this dick, ma. I like that. Beg for it."

"Please, daddy, let me suck your dick."

"You got it, mama."

He grabbed all of the pillows, fluffed them up, and laid back on them. His freaky ass wanted to watch me suck his dick, and he was going to get a movie because I missed this dick. He gripped his dick, and I kissed the head of it before I placed soft kisses up and down his shaft then taking the head of his dick in mouth and placing small bites on it.

"Ohhh, yeah. I like that, ma," Frank groaned.

I pulled back, spit on his dick, and started going up and down on it slowly.

"Move those fucking hands, and I better hear you gag on that shit," he ordered.

I put my hands behind my back and started deep throating him as best I could because I hadn't sucked his dick in a while. I went all the way down on his dick and held it in my mouth until I gagged on it. Slob was all over the base of his dick.

"Yeah, that's right. Gag all on that dick," he groaned. "You got that dick sloppy, bae."

Frank had a lot of dick, but I loved it and handled it like a pro. I kept gagging on his dick until tears were flowing down my eyes and my nose started running.

"Goddamn, you sucking this dick, beautiful."

Frank's face started turning red, and it looked like he was getting ready to bite his bottom lip off. I gagged on his dick one more time before I kissed down his shaft to suck on his balls. I put both of them in my mouth and started moving my head around, using my tongue to make circular motions. My mouth was so wet, and it was turning me on so bad. I could feel my juices seeping out of my pussy. Lifting Frank's balls with my face, I started to suck on his gooch lightly.

"Sssssssss..." he hissed.

Moments later, I felt warm liquid all over my face. Frank had cum, and it was getting all over the side of my face and all in my hair. That shit was spurting out like a broken water fountain, but I didn't stop until I got ready to. When I came up, he had his fist up to his mouth with his eyes closed, and he was shaking his head real slow. Nut was running down the sides of my face, getting on my titties and on the floor. It seemed like he shot out a cup of sperm.

"Frank... open your eyes," I whispered, but he shook his head.

"Girl. Girl. Girl. Girl. Girl. Girl," he repeated multiple times behind his closed fist.

"Frank... look at me."

He opened his eyes, and that nigga's eyes were misty and red like a mothafucka, making me lick my lips.

"That shit brought tears to my damn eyes. I swear I didn't mean to nut. My body did that shit on its own, man. You did that... and next thing I know... damn... nut was shooting through the head of my dick. Boy, head this good should be on display at a mothafuckin' museum," he said and closed his eyes again.

I got up and walked in the bathroom to clean my face up. This nigga had gotten nut all in my hair, and I was so thankful that I didn't have on one of my wigs, or I would have whooped his ass. When I walked back in the room, Frank was still lying in the same spot with his fist up to his mouth and his eyes closed. His dick was now laying flaccid on his thigh.

"Frank."

"Nah, Taiwan. I gotta process this shit. Give me about ten minutes. I need to figure out how the fuck my body just nutted like that. My bad for getting that on your face, but you looked sexy as shit with my jizz on your face."

Frank closed his eyes again and his fist started to weaken against his mouth and slowly fell to his side.

This nigga fell asleep, I thought to myself.

I smiled because I gave him an A for effort. I watched his chest rise and fall slowly. His body was perfect, and I couldn't help but to eye him. My heart stopped at the new tattoo he was sporting on his wrist that once donned Alex's name. It was 'Serenity' and a ladybug.

When the fuck did he get that? I thought to myself.

Lady bugs are supposed to be good luck, and I wondered if he got it while he was in Italy. It looked good as fuck etched into his skin. Whoever did the tattoo did a good ass job. I leaned over and kissed his cheek.

"Hmm," he groaned.

"Frank, I have to go. I have something to do, okay. I'll be back later today. Maybe we can finish what we started, okay."

His eyes popped open. "What you gotta do?"

"Girl shit, Frank."

He nodded his head and gripped my neck, pulling my lips to his. He pushed his tongue in my mouth, and we kissed for ten minutes straight. After we kissed, he smacked my ass, and then I got out of bed and left the guesthouse.

Why the fuck are doctor's offices always cold? I was so happy that I was called to the back after only being here thirty minutes. I had already finished peeing in the cup and getting my blood drawn. I was already in the room, waiting to get my first ultrasound. I couldn't wait to find out how far along I was. Moments later, a beautiful black woman doctor came in the room with a clipboard.

"I'm Dr. Alexis. How are you doing?"

"Great."

"All your paperwork points to you being pregnant. I'm going to do an ultrasound on you."

After the appointment was over, I was headed back toward Mayhem's house. I couldn't believe that I was eleven weeks pregnant. Frank had to have gotten me pregnant on my fucking birthday. I couldn't wait to get back to tell him. I was just going to show him the fucking ultrasound. I don't have a cute way to tell him. I pulled my phone out of my pocket, and I had twenty missed calls from Olena. I didn't even know that my phone was on silent. I called her back, and she picked up on the first ring.

"Taiwan, where the fuck are you!" Taiwan shouted into the phone.

"About twenty minutes away from the house. Why? What is going on?"

"Hurry up and get here! Frank just shot his parents, and now he's locked in the guesthouse with a gun to his head! Mayhem can't get him out! Please hurry!" Olena shouted into the phone and hung up.

WHAT THE FUCK!

FRANK

TEN MINUTES AFTER TAIWAN LEFT

After Taiwan left, I couldn't fall back asleep, so I got up to clean myself up and go holla at Mayhem. When I was in the bathroom, I was looking at myself in the mirror just to see if I had a soul left. Taiwan sucked my dick so goddamn good, and then the nerve of this girl to suck on my balls and then suck on my damn gooch. I swear I didn't even feel myself nutting until it was shooting through my head. Damn. She put me to mothafuckin' sleep. I'm marrying that damn girl. I don't give a fuck. Anytime a girl can suck your dick like that, make you nut, and put you to sleep, you gotta marry that mouth.

After I got myself cleaned up, I walked out of the bathroom and looked at the roses everywhere. I really tried to do something nice for Taiwan, but I clocked out after she sucked me to sleep. I knew that she was pissed after I left abruptly, but I almost hurt her. I needed to get away from Taiwan and handle that situation with Romero before he did more damage and I got even crazier. I couldn't believe that I almost hurt her the way that I did. I walked out of the guesthouse and up the path to Mayhem's house.

In the kitchen, Olena was fixing some food.

"I thought you was going with Taiwan," I said to Olena.

"Um, nope."

"Where is she? She said she was going to go do girl shit. I would think that y'all would be out doing girl shit together."

"She stepped out for a minute, Frank, dang. She's fine. Go down to the cave and take your mind off it before your bust your stitches," she said and laughed, but I didn't see shit funny.

I knew Olena knew where the hell she went, but I wasn't going to press the issue. Taiwan was going to have a lot of explaining to do when she got back here. If I felt like she was lying, I was just going to access the tracker I had on her phone. I limped down to Mayhem's mancave, and he was already rolling up. I needed some weed like yesterday because I hated the way the meds had me feeling, and I knew the weed would have me feeling good.

"You finally up and about, huh?" Mayhem stood and dapped me up.

"Hell yeah. I never did thank you for bringing Angel and Flash over here. You should have seen the look on her face," I said and eased down in the seat, and he sat across from me.

When I left Romero's house, I brought Angel and Flash with me and paid the people at the front a pretty penny to keep them, since I was about to do some dumb shit and didn't know if I would survive or not. I had even forgot to tell Mayhem about them being with the people at the front desk.

"Yeah. When we were getting ready to transport you back here, I went back to the spot we were staying at, and they asked me when you were going to be back to get them. I put them on the jet with us, and they were pretty cool. I figured that you would want to be the one to give them to her, so when we made it, I took them to that doggy hotel. Who the fuck knew a doggy hotel was the same damn price as a mothafuckin' hotel. I almost spazzed on that damn woman," Mayhem said and sparked up the blunt.

He puffed on it a few times before handing it to me. "I appreciate you like a mothafucka, man. Always having my back and shit. I would have been dead if you hadn't been there."

I puffed on the blunt a few times before handing it back to him.

"You ain't saying shit to me, man. I still ain't caught up to you on how many times you've saved my damn life. So, you good."

He passed the blunt back to me. "I remember when Lee killed your ass, and you said that you kept having dreams or something when you were in a coma. I ain't do none of that shit. I ain't feel shit. I ain't hear shit. None of that."

"Damn, that's wild. Everybody different. Are you supposed to be smoking?"

"Fine time to ask me, now." I pulled on the blunt and passed it back to him. "What I did hear is you talking to Alicia and telling her some shit. What were y'all talking about?"

"Not shit."

"Mayhem, don't bullshit me. What are y'all keeping from me? You know I don't play those jokes shit. What the fuck are y'all keeping from me?" I growled.

"Frank! Let's just not worry about it, aight. We about to be in a good place."

"Mayhem, if you don't tell me, I'm going to call her myself."

I pulled my phone out of my pocket and started typing on it.

"Man... I can't explain it. I don't want to explain it. I feel like you not in a place to know the information just yet."

"I'm calling her."

I called her and she picked up on the first ring.

"Frank!" she called my name in a dramatic whisper.

"A lot of noise in the background. Where you at? We need to talk."

"Mayhem told you?"

"He ain't told me shit. That's why I'm calling you."

"We have to talk face to face, Frank. This is something that we should speak about face to face."

"Oh. I'm not leaving the house for a lil' while. Come over here to my boy's crib. I'mma shoot you—"

"Nigga, that's a Fed. Are you crazy?"

"Tell Mr. Bailey I am leaving my retirement party now. This can't wait," she said and hung up.

"She is leaving her retirement party."

"I don't give a fuck, nigga."

I shrugged him off and typed in his address to Alicia.

Fifteen minutes later...

Me, Olena, Alicia, and Mayhem were sitting in the living room, looking at each other. She said the place where her party was being held was close to here, so it didn't take her long to make it. The kids were with Rubee in the playroom, so we could have this conversation with no kids involved.

"So... spit it out. Tell me what my nigga couldn't tell me," I urged her.

"This is going to sound strange, but—"

"Headline this story, ma'am."

"You're my nephew, and your real name is Malcolm Jr., not Frank," she rushed out.

"Nah, wrong person, fam. Nice chat though. My real name not even Frank... so."

"Frank... it's true," she said and paused. "When I first saw you, you reminded me so much of Malcolm Sr., and I just... haven't been able to get you off my mind since. It's you. I know it's you. Please don't be mad at me, Frank, but I had your blood tested while you were in a coma, and the DNA results say..." She paused and went her in bag, got a piece of paper out, and handed it to me. I damn near gave her a paper cut. "The DNA results says that we are related. So, you are my Malcolm Jr."

"This don't make no fucking sense to me. I was raised by my two parents in Memphis before I moved here at the age of fourteen. I'm not even from Chicago. Make this make sense before I snap your fucking neck," I growled.

"Okay. Okay."

She went in her bag again and pulled out a DVD, and she handed it to Olena. Olena got up and put the DVD in the system and grabbed the remote. She pressed play, and it looked like an old ass video from when camcorders first came out. On the screen was a pregnant white lady, and little white boy.

"That's not me!" I snapped.

"You're in the belly of my sister, Annette Bennett."

The camera stilled, and then a man came into the picture, and I had to turn my head because I was looking at my fucking self on the TV screen. That was me. Same head. Same body style. Same smile. He sat next to the pregnant lady and then laid his head on her belly.

"Malcolm Jr., I'm going to love you more than anything on this earth. Just like I love your mother and your brother. You're going to be strong... ehh, he kicked. Annette, he knows he's going to be strong. See."

"Turn it off!" I shouted.

I couldn't watch anymore. Suddenly, my life didn't make sense anymore. Olena turned the video off and took the DVD out and gave it back to Alicia.

"If I'm in her belly, with two loving parents, who *clearly* wanted me, how the fuck did I end up with two other parents then?"

She started reaching into her bag, but I stopped her. "Don't reach into your bag for shit else. Just... fucking tell me."

"Your father... your real father... Malcolm Sr., was a journalist. Everyone knew him. A very smart man, and that's what Annette loved the most about him. I believe that he came across something that he wasn't supposed to see, and he was killed. They killed him, Annette, and Joshua. They said that it was a murder suicide. I was like, how could it be a murder suicide when your body wasn't even found... nowhere. Nothing. It was like they didn't even look hard enough. I asked the police relentlessly about your missing case, but they actually wrote me off, and eventually I stopped asking. In my heart of hearts, I knew it was the government because one day, all of Malcolm Sr.'s articles were gone. You couldn't find any of them, nowhere. The only thing you could find was that he murdered his wife, son, and then himself."

After that information, I had to leave the house. I was not doubting Alicia because the evidence was right there in my face. I was the spitting image of my father. Spitting image. And I was half white, and I had a brother. All of that was right in my face. I left the house with Mayhem calling after me, but I ignored him and kept limping toward the guesthouse. Shit just didn't make sense, and the only person who knew the answer was the people I would probably never see again in life.

I walked in the guesthouse and slammed the door hard as hell. I walked further into the living room, and I almost lost my breath.

"Chaz, sit down," my father said.

I opened the drawer that was closest to me and grabbed my pistol. I cocked it, but I held it to my side. The way that I was feeling, I might shoot these mothafuckas who robbed me of a normal childhood.

"I don't feel like sitting down. What the fuck are you doing here? Why are you here now? Why now?"

"Well, you were going to get yourself killed, and we had to eliminate your enemies before they eliminated you first," my father said.

"And... we kind of have some explaining to do," my mother said softly.

I looked at them... stared at them. Twenty-two years had gone by, and they had barely aged. My dad's blemish free skin light skin still had a glow to it, and so did my mom's caramel colored skin. They hadn't gained any weight. They were in tip-top shape.

"It was you who shot Romero..." I said to confirm my suspicions.

"Of course. Did you think that we were going to let you go over to Italy and take on a cartel by yourself? Come on, now, Chaz. You are our son."

I pointed the gun at him. "No, don't you say that! I'm not your son."

"But you are, Chaz. We raised you. You belong to us. You were my son..." my mom said and started crying. "I knew the very day that white bitch approached Taiwan, she was going to be trouble. Please just let... please... let us explain."

"So you knew... about everything. You knew..." I paused.

My mother nodded her head. "Chaz, you have to understand—"

"What? What do I have to understand?"

"Put the gun down, and let's talk, son."

"Don't call me son! Don't fucking call me son!"

"Chaz, I always wanted to be a mother. I was recruited at eighteen, and by the time I was twenty, I realized that killing people for a living wasn't going to fulfill me. I wanted a child, but had I gotten pregnant, I would have been killed, so when Malcolm and his wife came across the radar..." she said and paused.

I started shaking my head. "No. No. No. No. No."

"Malcolm was starting to uncover secrets that would have been dangerous had it gotten out to the public and—"

"Get out!" I growled.

"You were in your crib and looked so peaceful. We were supposed to kill you as well, but you were just too perfect to kill. I saw it as my opportunity to—"

"GET OUT!"

"We were able to have somewhat of a normal family for fourteen years until it got out that we didn't complete the mission. That's why we had to go, Chaz."

"That's not my fucking name! You stole me from a perfect, loving family. I could have been anything, but look at me. You two raised me to be this psychotic, deranged individual. Because of the trauma you two put me through, I'm a burden to everyone around me. I can't sleep unless it's freezing cold in the room. I feel everything around me, even when I'm not supposed to. I almost broke my girl's arm not to long ago. People think I'm weird. The only people who really loved me were the people that's here."

"That's not true!" my mom yelled. "I loved you, Chaz! *We* loved and raised you the best way that we knew how."

"We are spies, son. How the fuck did you think we were supposed to raise you? To bake cookies like Annette and be in other people's business like Malcolm? Had we not raised you to be the person you are today, would you be a millionaire? Granted, you get it by selling drugs, but you are rich nonetheless."

"My life would have been better than waking up in sweats every other night, dreaming about being in the box that the monster you sent me to live with put me in. My life would have been better than thinking killing people is normal or locking them in cages is normal. My life would have been much better than that, I can tell you that."

"Oh please, Chaz—"

"That's not my fucking name!"

"You were only Malcolm Jr. for two months," my dad said. "Look, Malcolm Sr. was broke. You would have woken up to bugs crawling all over you in the cardboard box that you were about to be living in. They were broke, and—"

"Russell," my mom whispered and touched his knee.

"Russell is your name? And what is your name, *mother*?"

"Joan."

I nodded my head and chuckled.

"The only reason that we are here is because your mother—"

"She's not my…"

Before I could finish my sentence, I blacked out.

Pow! Pow! Pow! Pow!

I shot both of them twice in their stomachs. I shot them perfectly so they would die slowly. I walked over to the door and barricaded the door because I knew that Mayhem was on his way back here. I walked back over to them, and they were both holding on to their wounds for dear life.

"See! This is who you made me!" I growled.

"This…" I pointed the barrel of the gun in my chest. "This is who you two made me into. A killer. A coldblooded killer."

Boom! Boom! Boom!

"Frank! What the fuck? Open the fucking door. What the fuck is going on in there!" Mayhem yelled on the outside of the door while trying to knock it in.

BIANCA JONES

They both were spitting up blood, and for the first time, I felt something... Sorrow. Tears sprang into my eyes because I couldn't believe this shit. They kidnapped me and raised me into this monster and was proud of it.

"I love... I love you, Chaz," Joan muttered.

"Shut the fuck up! That's not my name!" I shouted.

Pow!

I shot her in the head.

BOOM! BOOM! BOOM!

"FRANK! FRANK! What the fuck is going on in there!" Mayhem yelled outside the door.

I watched as Russell choked on his own blood until he took his last breath. Tears slowly rolled down my eyes as I went and took a seat on the floor in front of the shit I barricaded the door with. I was tired. My whole life was a lie. Everything about my life was a lie. I wasn't Frank. I wasn't even Chaz. I was Malcolm Bennett, Jr., son of a journalist. Son of a homemaker. I had a brother. I was half-white. I was kidnapped. How the fuck was I supposed to wanna live after this shit here.

"Frank!" Mayhem shouted on the other side of the door.

"I'm tired, Mayhem," I replied and put the gun to my head. "I'm just gonna do it."

"What are you tired of, Frank? Open the door, buddy, so we can talk."

"I'm tired of talking, Mayhem. This shit just not fair. My whole life is a lie."

"Open the door so we can talk. Why did I hear gunshots, Frank?"

"My parents were here. In here. I shot them. They confirmed everything. I was kidnapped, Mayhem."

"Frank, I get it. Open the door so we can talk, please."

"I'm tired. I just feel like dying. Leave me alone, Mayhem."

"I'll tell you what, Frank. Let's do it together. I can't live without you, brother. So count off and we can do it together. I have my gun to my head right now."

Olena let out a blood curdling scream, which let me know that he wasn't lying.

"You got my nephew and nieces. Don't do that. That'll be stupid. Olena will be devastated."

"So me killing myself is stupid but you killing yourself ain't. Frank. Open this door."

"My whole life was a lie. I'm tired of being a burden to you, Mayhem, and your family. Y'all don't deserve this. I can't take no more disappointments, brother."

He was quiet.

"Frank, please come out here. My husband is out here with a gun to his head because you have one to yours… and I just can't live without either one of you. Who's going to make jokes about my kids' big heads every day? Who's going to protect Mayhem? Who's going to make him laugh on the days I pissed him off? Who's going to love Taiwan? Did you think about how this would kill her?"

Taiwan. Where the fuck is she? Another fucking disappointment. She can't handle being with me anyway.

"Frank, you're about to be a father…" Olena said. "You're going to be a father. Taiwan's giving you your first child. Don't you want to be here to see him or her born?"

"No she's not. You're just saying that. She's not pregnant. She would have told me if she was pregnant. Go away, Lee."

"On your count, Frank," Mayhem said.

"Pryor!" Olena screamed his name.

"One…" Mayhem counted.

"Don't do this, Mayhem. You have shit to live for. I fucking don't."

"Yes the fuck you do, nigga. Me. Live for me! Live for your nieces and nephews. Live for your fucking parents, Paxton and Angela Bailey. They are your parents, Frank. Did you think about how that would make your old man feel, having to scrape your brains up off the floor? They love you unconditionally. You are his son, Frank. You want me to call him?"

"No."

"Well, let's get it over with, Frank. Two," Mayhem counted. "We can do it together. Our parents are just going to have to lose two sons in one day. They'll have Malice left."

"Don't do it, Mayhem! Put it down. Just let me do this!"

"Don't you do it, Frank."

Knock! Knock! Knock!

"Frank... it's me, Taiwan," she said outside the door.

It sounded like she was out of breath.

"Go away, Taiwan."

I swatted at the tears and snot that were flowing like a river down my face.

"Can I give you something... before you do it? I just want to show you this, and then after I show you this, I want to tell you something," she said.

"Slide it under the door."

Moments later, I heard something slide under the door. I turned around and picked up the soft piece of paper. I studied the paper and my lips turned up a little. She is pregnant. Her name was at the top of the paper, so I knew the paper wasn't fake.

"Frank... I understand you. I love you. A lot. I'd be really sad if I had to raise our child without his or her daddy. I won't be able to tell stories the way that you can. I don't have big strong arms like you that will be able to cradle the baby. We can get through this together, okay. I won't judge you. You won't have to bear the burden alone. If you let me love you the way that you need to be loved, you'll be able to take on the world. I can't protect our child by myself. I'm just not strong enough. You're my protector, Frank. Who's going to hold my hand when I'm delivering the baby? You have a chance to finally be the father that you never had. If it's a girl, you can teach them how to jump rope. If it's a boy, you can teach them how to hunt. Bottom line, Frank, I need you. We need you. Everybody out here needs you. On days like this, Frank, I'll be strong for you. Please open the door and let me be strong for you."

I got quiet as I continued to stare at my baby on this ultrasound. I stood up and moved the stuff out of the way. I opened the door slightly, and I saw everyone outside with tears running down their eyes, and Mayhem had his gun at his side. Taiwan was standing there, looking up at me with red eyes. She held her hand out, and it was shaking. As scared as she was, she was still trying to be strong for me. I placed my hand in her small shaky hand, and she placed it on her stomach. Her stomach was still soft.

"This is our baby, Frank. We made this baby out of love, right?" she asked me.

I nodded my head.

"Give me the gun, Franklin."

Reluctantly, I opened the door wider and handed her the gun. After I handed it to her, she handed it to Mayhem. I fell into her arms, and we slowly slid to the ground. I had my head in her chest, and I cried.

"We are going to be good. I promise. We are going to get past this," she whispered in my ear.

"I believe you, Serenity."

EPILOGUE

NINE MONTHS LATER

Rubee

Kade and I were staring down at our bundle of joy, Kade Lewis Jr., in his crib after I had finished feeding him and putting him to sleep. He was beautiful and looked exactly like his father. These last nine months have been everything that I never would have imagined I'd have. Since that first time Bash called me, I never heard from him again. I didn't know where he was, and I didn't care. Raylee didn't even ask about him anymore, and that was a good thing.

"Mrs. Lewis, how did you give me something so beautiful?" Kade asked me.

"I'll never get enough of hearing that, Mr. Lewis. I can't believe we made him."

Kade and I had a small ceremony three months ago, with our family and friends included, and even though I was big and pregnant, I looked amazing. We flew down to Texas two weeks after we announced my pregnancy to my uncle and aunt, to tell my parents, and it went exactly how my uncle said it would. My dad was pissed about me being pregnant. He was pissed about Kade being older than me. No matter what Kade said, it wasn't good enough for him. After Kade put him in his place, we left the house, and my parents didn't talk to me for months. I could have cried when my dad showed up to give me away to Kade. After the wedding, my parents stayed with us for a couple of weeks to help me prepare for the baby, and it was something. Even my dad and uncle had a good time with each other. I thought I would never see the day.

"When are you going back to work?" I asked him.

"Maybe in about three more weeks. I want to be at home with you three all the time. Mayhem understands, and plus, I can work from home on most things."

"I love having you here. I ordered a camera, and it came in, so we have to go pick it up soon," I said to him.

"Okay. Let me go get Raylee ready."

Raylee and Kade got along so well, sometimes better than her little self got along with me. They were always cooking together. I think she liked cooking with him because he still let her use knives. She didn't like cooking with me because I was not patient enough to let her use a knife with me. When I looked at my little family, I couldn't believe that God blessed me the way that He did. People really come in your life for a reason. Kade came into my life, and he changed it drastically. He loved me more than I love myself sometimes. He was a great dad to Raylee. With him, I found myself being calm about everything. I was not as angry as I used to be. The sex was still amazing. Sometimes, I got in my own feelings and wondered if he'd leave me because I was cheating on my boyfriend with him, and he swiftly reminded me that he didn't put these five karats on my finger to cheat on me.

My stylist company was doing well. In nine months, I had gained twenty thousand followers. I had even styled and photographed some of these new Chicago rappers. My business started booming so well that I had to get my own studio to keep all my equipment. Even though Kade was skeptical about me opening my business up more while I was pregnant, he still supported me 1,000 percent, like he said he would. I was also Taiwan's photographer for her pictures and shit, and she paid me good. Kade told me when I found something that I loved to do, it would never feel like work.

It felt good to feel secure in your relationship. I never had the urge to go through his phone or follow him places. Kade didn't let anyone disrespect me, and he blocked girls on his social media that tried to holla at him. Kade was really the man of my dreams. People could say Kade and I moved fast, but when you knew what you wanted, it wasn't no time limit.

TAIWAN

TAIWAN

It has been a wild nine months, but we made it through. After Frank had his nervous breakdown, he realized that he needed some type of help. He started going to Mayhem's therapist once a week, and it helped him a lot. A whole lot. He seemed much happier these days, and I loved that about him. The therapist recommended medication, but he said that he wasn't going to take any medication, and I supported any decision that he made.

We finally moved back into his home, and I had stripped his house clean of Alex ever being there. It was like she was never there. We got all new furniture, and he turned that box room into his man cave. I told him that I was not going to be living in a house knowing that there were cages and other shit that once held me and another woman in there. We fought about it for weeks, but he finally had that room changed into his man cave.

I had just put on a bathing suit and walked into the room where Frank was laying in the bed on his back with his left arm stretched out, and Fallyn Serene Bailey Ward, our daughter, was laying her little head on his bicep. Frank wanted to name her after the Bailey's and since Bailey can be a girl name, I put it as one of her middle names. She had her little booty in the air and was sucking on her little fist while looking upside her dad's head while he watched TV. It was funny how the universe worked. Fallyn came out looking like Frank's mom, Annette. Had Frank never found out about his birth parents, he probably would have killed me. She had a head full of thick curls that I was not going to know how to comb when the time came.

"You are looking fly, mama. You getting ready to have a photoshoot? Rubee coming over?"

"Oh nah. I just have to take a couple of pics for Instagram for this boutique."

When I was four months pregnant, I completely rebranded. *TaiDFashions* was no more because I felt like that name was tied to Romero, because most of my photos were taken in Italy. My new name was now *SerenetheFashionFoodie*, and over 90 percent of the people from *TaiDFashions* had followed me right over, which meant I had my millions of followers back with the quickness. I had a blog about motherhood, food, and fashion. Sometimes my blogs were featured in magazines, which brought me more followers. I couldn't believe this was my life.

I held the camera up to take the beautiful picture of Fallyn looking up at her daddy. She loved her daddy so much, and his bicep was her favorite spot to lay. I snapped the picture, and he looked at me.

"Let me see how I look because you know you be posting me when I be looking foolish," he said.

"Frank… you think because you got a lil' hive, you all that. You ain't shit," I said and laughed.

Sometimes when I go live, Frank be with me, and my followers loved him. They loved when I went live with him on social media, and it was funny that they thought he be playing when he said some of the shit that he said, but he'd be dead serious.

"Mane, I just like to look good, chill out."

"I'm going to be out back."

"Alright. I'mma be chilling with my shorty."

Once I was out back, Angel and Flash ran up to me, and I rubbed them. Not a day went by where I didn't think about my parents and if they forgave me for choosing Romero over them. It sucked that I'd never know if they did or not. Frank told me that he learned in therapy that he didn't need to focus on the things that he couldn't change. One good thing that came from this was the fact that I do talk to Tristan every day. Alicia got his time cut, and he should be out in about six months. They even sent him to a work release program, and that made me happy.

Life was good for me. I had the man of my dreams. Don't get me wrong, Frank was still off his rocker, but he'd calmed down a lot. Since I'd had the baby, he'd been home more, and I loved that. He never wanted to leave Fallyn's side. He watched her while she slept because he was afraid that he may miss something. I could post anything on my blog, but not *his* daughter. He said because if he saw one bad comment, he wouldn't hesitate to go to their house and fuck that person up, so I respected his wishes. For me, life was great.

FRANK

FRANK

What a nigga like me do to deserve all of this?

A girl that loved the fuck out of my dirty briefs.

A family that's been supportive of me since the day that I met them.

A lot of zeroes in my bank account.

God was tripping when He gave a crazy nigga like me a daughter, but I still didn't feel like I deserved all of this.

The day I held that gun to my head but didn't pull the trigger, I knew I needed help. Mayhem convinced me to see his therapist, and at first, I was reluctant, but I finally went. He changed my life in more ways than one, to be honest. Since I'd been seeing him, I learned how to love Taiwan better. Yes, I love her. My actions showed that I loved her, but I didn't tell her until the day she pushed out my daughter. Mayhem told me that I would be overcome with emotions when I saw her pop out, and I was. My eyes got misty like a mothafucka. Seeing Taiwan pop my baby out with no fucking medication, I had no choice but to let my shorty know that she was much stronger than I'd ever be and that I loved her. I think she cried harder because I told her that I loved her.

I learned to love myself through my therapist. I was being hard on myself over things I had no control of. I had no control over my birth parents and brother being murdered. I had no control over Russell and Joan kidnapping me and raising me to be the person I am. I had no control over any of that, so I shouldn't beat myself up about it. The only thing I had control over was my anger and my actions in the future. He wanted me to take pills, but that was a no no. I wasn't going to put nothing in my body that was going to alter the way I think.

Another reason why I knew I'd changed because I'd put finding Alex, Bash, and Kharisma on hold to be a better lover and a father. It was just not a high priority for me anymore. I told my therapist that I'd put it on hold, but if I did see them, then they were leaving this earth, and that was point, blank, period. I even let Miguel go home to his mother down in Florida, however, I told him, if he stepped one foot in Chicago, it would be curtains for him. He told me that I didn't have to tell him twice.

Alicia. Over the last nine months, we'd talked a lot. I'd met her husband, her kids, and their kids. They were a nice family, and I was slowly but surely getting close to them. Alicia had so many pictures of my mom and dad. I had a picture of my birth parents and me as a kid, sitting on the entertainment system in my man cave. For some odd reason, it made me feel like they were watching over me. I hated that I found out about my birth parents the way that I did, but my therapist said that it was something that I needed to know to help me heal properly. Sometimes I wonder what my life would have been like had I been raised by my birth parents, but then I shake away the thoughts because I definitely wouldn't have met a great family like the Bailey's. Since I had been Frank since I was fourteen, I wasn't going to change that shit.

I may have real love in my life. God, I loved Taiwan's beautiful brown ass.

I may have my beautiful daughter in my life. Yes, I will kill you over her. Without question.

I may have a piece of my birth family in my life now. They real cool too.

BIANCA JONES

I may have even taken the person who double crossed me off my high priority list.

I may have even shed a tear or two within the last few months.

With all of that, please don't you ever forget, that I am still one insane mothafucka.

The End

MESSAGE FROM THE AUTHOR

This series has finally come to an end. I would like to thank all of you who were patient with me as I closed out this series. I know a lot of you may be upset about Alex and Bash not getting 'got', but just keep in mind that Frank did remind y'all at the end, he may have changed, but he is still **InSANE.** Catch those teas.

Pllllleeeaaase leave a review and let me know how you liked it.

Bianca Xaviera
LoveTheBeeXWay

ABOUT THE AUTHOR

Bianca was born and raised in a small town called Lake Village, AR. She attended college at the University of Central Arkansas where she obtained a degree in Health Education. After graduating in 2014 she relocated to Jacksonville, FL where she works as a Medical Office Coordinator at Florida Counseling and Evaluations.

STAY CONNECTED:
Join
Bee's Literary Beehive Readers Group

Subscribe to my Website for Sneak Peeks & More: Authoress Bianca

facebook.com/AuthoressBianca
instagram.com/BiancaXaviera_

ALSO BY AUTHORESS BIANCA

Fallin' For A Black Billionaire

A Mayhem Love 1-3

A Malice 1-3

Scorpion & Zolar: A Dangerous Gangsta Love

Her Heart & His Crown 1-3

Can't Hide From Love 1-4

Love Comes With A Price 1-3

Love Conquers All 1-3

Fallin' For The Enemy: A Love That Wasn't Supposed To Be

You Ain't Gotta Be Perfect 1-3

I'll Always Belong To You 1-2 (Collab)

Phresh & Nykee: Loving You Past The Pain 1-3

Royalty Publishing House is now accepting manuscripts from aspiring or experienced urban romance authors!

WHAT MAY PLACE YOU ABOVE THE REST:

Heroes who are the ultimate book bae: strong-willed, maybe a little rough around the edges but willing to risk it all for the woman he loves.

Heroines who are the ultimate match: the girl next door type, not perfect - has her faults but is still a decent person. One who is willing to risk it all for the man she loves.

The rest is up to you! Just be creative, think out of the box, keep it sexy and intriguing!

If you'd like to join the Royal family, send us the first 15K words (60 pages) of your completed manuscript to submissions@royaltypublishinghouse.com

LIKE OUR PAGE!

Be sure to LIKE our Royalty Publishing House page on Facebook!